the challenge

Prince Jen raised the sword point. Seeing their chief threatened, a couple of Natha's companions started forward. Natha waved them away. "We have a fighting cricket here. I can deal with him."

Natha's hand went to his own sword hilt. Prince Jen crouched, ready for the attack. Natha drew out only the jagged stump of a blade.

"I broke this against those Kwan-tzu yokels." Natha tossed aside the shattered weapon. "I must have another. You can't expect me to go unarmed"—Natha spread his empty hands—"not in my trade. We can settle the matter reasonably between us."

Prince Jen had been well instructed in swordplay, but Natha suddenly leaped faster than his eyes could follow. He swung the blade wildly, borne back against the cavern wall. In the instant, Natha seized him by the hair with one hand and by the throat with the other.

"Here's the nub of it," Natha said through clenched teeth. "You try a stab at me. If you can. The question: Will you do it before I snap your neck? Think it over. Quickly. You manage to put that blade in my belly? Do you suppose my people would let you or your friends out of here alive?"

BOOKS BY LLOYD ALEXANDER

The Chronicles of Prydain

The Book of Three

The Black Cauldron

The Castle of Llyr

Taran Wanderer

The High King

The Foundling

The Westmark Trilogy

Westmark

The Kestrel

The Beggar Queen

The Vesper Holly Adventures

The Illyrian Adventure

The El Dorado Adventure

The Drackenberg Adventure

The Jedera Adventure

The Philadelphia Adventure

The Xanadu Adventure

Other Books

LLOYD ALEXANDER

The Remarkable Journey of Prince Jen

PUFFIN BOOKS

PUFFIN BOOKS

Published by the Penguin Group

Penguin Young Readers Group, 345 Hudson Street, New York, New York 10014, U.S.A.

Penguin Group (Canada), 10 Alcorn Avenue, Toronto, Ontario, Canada M4V 3B2

(a division of Pearson Penguin Canada Inc.)

Penguin Books Ltd, 80 Strand, London WC2R 0RL, England

Penguin Ireland, 25 St Stephen's Green, Dublin 2, Ireland

(a division of Penguin Books Ltd)

Penguin Group (Australia), 250 Camberwell Road, Camberwell, Victoria 3124, Australia

(a division of Pearson Australia Group Pty Ltd)

Penguin Books India Pvt Ltd, 11 Community Centre, Panchsheel Park,

New Delhi - 110 017, India

Penguin Group (NZ), Cnr Airborne and Rosedale Roads, Albany, Auckland,

New Zealand (a division of Pearson New Zealand Ltd)

Penguin Books (South Africa) (Pty) Ltd, 24 Sturdee Avenue, Rosebank,

Johannesburg 2196, South Africa

Registered Offices: Penguin Books Ltd, 80 Strand, London WC2R 0RL, England

First published in the United States of America by Dutton Children's Books,
a division of Penguin Books USA Inc., 1991

Published by Puffin Books, a division of Penguin Young Readers Group, 2004

3 5 7 9 10 8 6 4

THE LIBRARY OF CONGRESS HAS CATALOGED THE DUTTON EDITION AS FOLLOWS:

Alexander, Lloyd.

The remarkable journey of Prince Jen / Lloyd Alexander.

p.   cm.

Summary: Bearing six unusual gifts, young Prince Jen embarks on
a perilous quest and emerges triumphantly into manhood.

ISBN 0-525-44826-8

[1. Adventure and adventurers—Fiction. 2. Princes—Fiction. 3. Fantasy.] I. Title.

PZ7.A3774Re   1991   91-13720

[Fic]—dc20   CIP   AC

Puffin Books ISBN 0-14-240225-7

Printed in the United States of America

You must know nothing before
you can learn something,
and be empty
before you can be filled.

—MASTER SHU

· Contents ·

the
Remarkable Journey
of Prince Jen

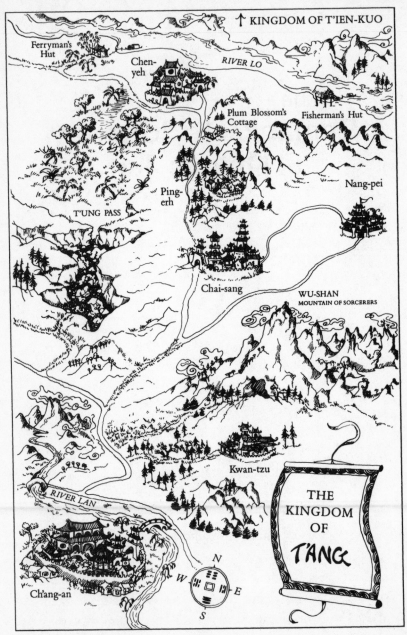

Map by Debby L. Carter

1

ONE MORNING, A RAGGED OLD MAN came hobbling
to the Jade Gate of the Celestial Palace in Ch'ang-an.
He leaned on a staff, his robe was kilted to his knees,
red dust caked his bare feet. He was not a beggar, since
he asked for no alms. He was not a man of wisdom,
since he did something ridiculous: He demanded an audience with King T'ai.

The guards would have had rough sport with the
foolish old fellow, but the look in his eyes made them
uneasy and uncertain what to do about him. So, they

reported his presence to the Department of Further Study. There, the officials decided that he was merely a wandering lunatic and should receive five blows from the Rod of Correction. However, when the guards returned to administer Benign Chastisement, he had vanished.

Later that day, Young Lord Prince Jen was practicing archery at the far end of Spring Blossom Garden. It was one of his many accomplishments, which included appreciation of the new moon at the Mid-Autumn Festival, riding, fencing, writing poetry, and knowledge of the Six Forms of Polite Address, the Eight Mandarin Ranks, and other essential information.

His servant, a round-faced, bandy-legged fellow named Mafoo, had gone to retrieve an arrow when Prince Jen glimpsed an astonishing sight: an intruder on the palace grounds. At first, Jen thought it was his beloved old teacher, Master Hu, who had instructed him in Princely Virtues, as well as all the other precepts, principles, and analects that a young man of Jen's rank was required to know. Jen and the ancient sage had been devoted to each other. One day, however, Master Hu disappeared from the palace and never returned.

It was not Master Hu. Unhindered by walls, gates, and sentries, a stranger was making his way across the gardens toward the Pavilion of Joyful Mornings, where the ailing King T'ai customarily took the fresh air.

Prince Jen immediately summoned Mafoo, who peered in the direction his master indicated.

"Do you mean that old codger in a red robe?" Mafoo said, squinting one eye, then the other. "Carrying a walking staff? Prosperous, distinguished looking, with a long white beard?"

"Exactly," Jen said.

"I see nothing at all," Mafoo said. "Since it's not allowed, he isn't there. He's a figment of your imagination."

"You see him as well as I do," Jen said, hustling Mafoo toward the pavilion. "Don't play the fool."

"Who's playing?" Mafoo muttered. "This is something out of the ordinary. I've served long enough in the palace to know one thing: What starts by being unusual ends by being troublesome."

Jen's astonishment grew. Outside the pavilion, instead of rushing to protect King T'ai, the royal bodyguards stood about in befuddlement. Some leisurely scratched themselves, others stared blankly at the clouds. A few had gone to sleep on their feet and snored loudly.

Jen hurried into the pavilion. There sat his father conversing with a lean old man whose weathered face was brown and wrinkled as a walnut shell.

"My son, how surprising this is," King T'ai said. "I was about to send for you this very moment. Here is Master Wu. He has journeyed great distances and learned much of interest to me during his travels. I confess he so startled me at first that I feared I must have died without noticing it and he was a spirit come to lead me to my ancestors. I could only wish he had chosen a more conventional way of obtaining an audience."

"With all honor and respect, Your Highness," replied Master Wu, "had I done so, would it have been granted? I understand an old man of the streets sought a hearing but was sentenced to a beating."

"If so, I regret it," said King T'ai. "I know nothing of him. My councillors decide who is admitted into my presence. As for yourself, Master Wu, you seem a person of substance and rank. Your request would surely have been given every consideration."

"Perhaps, or perhaps not," Master Wu said. "Yet, as the poet Lo Yih-tsi wrote:

> Whether it comes wrapped
> In fresh leaves or old straw,
> The discerning cook smiles and says,
> 'What an excellent fish!' "

Master Wu now turned his attention to Prince Jen. The wayfarer did not fling himself to his knees and knock his head on the ground, as the law required. After a calculating glance, he nodded briefly.

"I was speaking to His Majesty," Master Wu said, "of a happy, harmonious realm."

"Clearly," Mafoo said under his breath to Jen, "the old geezer doesn't mean our Kingdom of T'ang."

"The old geezer," said Master Wu, whose ears must

have been as sharp as his eyes, "was referring to the Kingdom of T'ien-kuo."

"Is there truly such a place?" asked Prince Jen. Long ago, Master Hu had spoken of T'ien-kuo, but the old sage himself was not certain whether it existed or was only a fairy tale.

"So I gather, from all I have heard and read," Master Wu said. "It is a remarkable kingdom. Far north of here, in its great capital, Ch'ung-chao, reigns the noblest and most generous of rulers: Yuan-ming. His subjects thrive and prosper, the land yields harvests in abundance, the arts flourish as richly as the orchards. The laws are just, but seldom enforced, since the inhabitants deal with each other as they themselves would wish to be dealt with. Thus, few officials are needed, but they serve their monarch and the people well."

"If true," Jen said, "it must be the Sphere of Heavenly Perfection itself."

Master Wu chuckled like a dry branch scraping a roof. "Indeed not. How could it be? Even in T'ien-kuo, none can escape living or dying, the pains of rheumatism or the pangs of a broken heart. There, simply, a reasonable amount of happiness is a definite possibility."

"I would be glad for half as much in my own kingdom," said King T'ai. "I wish to consult Yuan-ming and learn how he governs his people. I have little strength for a long journey, but I must make it nevertheless."

Prince Jen was about to speak, but Mafoo dropped

to his knees before the king. "Divine Majesty, I offer a humble suggestion. The journey will be difficult, uncomfortable to say the least, with who knows what dangers. Send someone else to observe Yuan-ming's methods and principles. Give the task to the lowest-ranking official in the palace. If something fatal happens to him, he won't be missed. Better yet, send a high official, who will be missed even less."

"Would they report the truth to me?" replied the king. "I doubt it. They would tell me what they wished me to hear, for their own benefit. Who goes in my place must be one I trust beyond question."

"Honored Father," Prince Jen began, "hear my own thought."

"Young Lord, be careful," Mafoo whispered. "I know you're good-hearted, well-meaning, kindly, with a sweet and innocent nature. Therefore, you're about to do something stupid."

"Honored Father," Jen continued, "let me make the journey."

"I knew it!" groaned Mafoo. "Young Lord, you've never set foot outside the palace grounds. You've never put on your clothes for yourself, or even washed your own feet. For your own good, avoid such a journey."

Prince Jen, despite Mafoo tugging at his sleeve, went on so eagerly and persuasively that King T'ai nodded agreement.

"Go, then. Study and learn all that is possible. If Yuan-ming is as generous as Master Wu tells us, he will surely welcome you and share his wisdom. I will anxiously await your return."

"Young Lord," whispered Mafoo, "will you give your groveling servant permission to speak?"

"Mafoo," said Prince Jen, "first, when have you ever groveled? Second, when have you ever asked permission for anything?"

"Young Lord," said Mafoo, "I haven't told you this before, but I have to tell you now. No one could hope for a better master than your noble self. Since your revered mother passed away, I have served you with admiration and affection growing greater every day. The thought of your leaving on such a journey is more than I can bear. Therefore, I beg you: Stay in the palace. Find someone else to undertake the hardships."

"Good Mafoo!" cried Prince Jen. "Faithful Mafoo! What you have said touches me deeply. I had no idea you would be so grieved by my absence. I cannot bring myself to put such a painful burden on your loyal heart."

"Blessings on you," exclaimed Mafoo. "I knew I could count on your kindness and compassion."

"You can," said Prince Jen. "Therefore, I have decided to take you with me."

"What?" Mafoo clapped his hands to his head. "Young Lord, do you realize——?"

"So be it," said King T'ai. "What better companion than one who declares such deep devotion?"

"Your Highness," Mafoo said hastily, "there has

been a small misunderstanding. I only wanted to protect the Young Lord."

"So you shall," said King T'ai. "I count on your affection and obedience. I have every confidence you will not let Prince Jen come to harm. See to his comfort as you would your own."

"Of that," answered Mafoo, "you can be absolutely certain."

"Make preparations now," declared King T'ai. "I will order an escort of my finest troops, and write a royal warrant, stamped with my vermilion seal, commanding every subject, every official throughout the land to provide all that Prince Jen may require."

"Wait." Master Wu raised a hand. "There is one difficulty."

*   *   *   *   *

Our young hero is eager to start his journey, but Master Wu seems to be casting a dark shadow on a bright prospect. What can be the difficulty? To find out, read the next chapter.

2

JEN'S FACE FELL. He stared in dismay at Master Wu. "But—all is settled. What difficulty can there be?"

"Finding suitable gifts," replied Master Wu. "All who seek an audience with Yuan-ming must bring him worthy offerings. Not to do so would be a most profound discourtesy, a mortal affront. Yuan-ming is a kindly, reasonable monarch, but on this point I understand he is unshakable. Without acceptable tokens of esteem, Young Lord, you would surely be turned away."

"That difficulty is easily overcome," said King T'ai.

"I will open the Hall of Priceless Treasures and hold back nothing that may please Yuan-ming."

Jen's concern vanished. "Only a matter of costly presents? Master Wu, you'll find more than enough."

"Perhaps," Master Wu said. "We shall see." He turned to the king. "I must be allowed to choose the gifts, without question or objection to what I select."

King T'ai nodded. "I put all my possessions at your disposal."

The guards by now had recovered from their befuddlement and rushed into the pavilion. King T'ai gestured for them to lower their swords and lances. He ordered their captain to carry word to General Li Kwang, the king's commander of palace troops. Li Kwang was to attend him later in the Chamber of Private Discourses; meantime, he was to assemble a princely escort of horsemen and foot soldiers, holding them ready to depart for the Kingdom of T'ien-kuo at the earliest moment.

From the Pavilion of Joyful Mornings, the king led Master Wu, Prince Jen, and Mafoo to the Hall of Priceless Treasures. The surprised First Custodian unlocked the teakwood cabinets, opened huge golden coffers, and drew back the silken drapes from the alcoves. Master Wu glanced around him as the Second and Third Custodians scurried ahead to unbar other chambers.

Even as Master Wu began peering at the store of treasures, news of the king's intention spread from one department to the next.

The highest officials urged King T'ai to give up his ill-considered, ill-advised, and impossible plan. For once, the king refused to heed them. If they thwarted his wishes, he warned them, every official in the palace would be demoted by two grades. They fell silent instantly.

Meanwhile, Master Wu continued inspecting the royal treasures. For three days, he paced the chambers and galleries. Each day, Prince Jen grew more dismayed. Master Wu shrugged at the priceless figurines of rare jade. He wrinkled his nose at the exquisite porcelain ware and waved a scornful hand at the intricate objects of pure gold.

When King T'ai came to learn the reason for the delay, Master Wu shook his head.

"Among all these treasures," he declared, as Prince Jen's heart sank, "I find none worthy of offering to Yuan-ming."

One chamber remained unexamined. The First Custodian assured the king that it held items of little value or interest. They had not been sorted, listed, or classified and hardly merited even counting as part of the royal collection.

"Let me look at them nevertheless," Master Wu said.

Following him into this last chamber, Prince Jen glimpsed only a hodgepodge of dust-covered articles. He was about to turn away, disappointed, when Master Wu's eyes brightened.

"Here—yes, here is one acceptable gift." He pointed

to a curved sword leaning in a corner. The First Custodian hastened to fetch it. Master Wu stepped toward a pile of harness leathers, stirrups, and other gear.

"There is a saddle," he said. "I choose it as well."

From then on, Master Wu unhesitatingly selected one item after the other, though his choices struck Prince Jen as being of much less value than the treasures in the other chambers. In addition to the first two, Master Wu rummaged out four more. He bobbed his head and pronounced himself satisfied. The First Custodian begged to mention that a list must be made of any objects removed. He produced a tablet of paper and wrote according to Master Wu's direction:

Item: one sword, iron, with scabbard likewise, including tassels and attaching rings.

Item: a saddle, of tooled leather, with stirrups and bridle.

Item: a flute, of painted wood.

Item: a bowl, bronze, one handspan in circumference.

Item: a box, of sandalwood, containing one paintbrush, one ink stick, and one ink stone for grinding same.

Item: one kite, paper, bird-shaped, with wooden rods and struts (disassembled), including one ball of string.

"A child's toy?" Prince Jen, hearing this last object named, whispered to Mafoo. "What value does this have for Yuan-ming? Can Master Wu be serious?"

Mafoo shrugged. "At least it's easy to carry. What if the old bird had picked a pair of ten-foot vases?"

General Li Kwang had done his king's bidding perfectly. Assembled in the palace courtyard the next morning, a splendid escort of cavalry and foot soldiers stood ready while Prince Jen knelt to take leave of his father. He had expected Master Wu to be on hand to offer parting words of advice, but the old man was nowhere to be found.

The six chosen objects had been wrapped in silk and set beside Prince Jen in a carriage canopied in yellow brocade. Mafoo had appointed himself driver of the pair of white horses. The Jade Gate was flung open. Tall banners fluttering, tassels swinging at the necks of the steeds, horsehair plumes waving at the crests of glittering helmets, the procession crossed the Great Square of Tranquil Harmony. Word of Prince Jen's purpose had been cried throughout Ch'ang-an. As the carriage passed, the townspeople dropped to their knees and called down ten thousand blessings on the journey.

As for Prince Jen, his long hair bound up under a tall cap stiff with gold embroidery, his robes wrapped around him and tied with a sash at his waist, he composed his features in a look of calm dignity, as he had always been instructed to do. However, with the cheers of the townsfolk ringing in his ears, he found this attitude more and more difficult.

"Has there ever been a day like this?" he cried. "Has the sky ever been so blue? Or the sun so bright? The air has a fragrance I never smelled in the palace. What is this spicy perfume?"

"Let me analyze it." Mafoo sniffed loudly. "Ah. Yes. I can identify the subtle ingredients. One part fried cabbage. One part wandering livestock. Two parts old rags. Four parts sweat. The rest, a concentrated absence of cash. Mixed with the correct proportions of thievery, beggary, and a generous pinch of greedy officials, it is called 'Sublime Essence of Wretchedness.' "

"You make sport of my ignorance," Prince Jen said reproachfully.

"No, no," Mafoo protested. "Ignorance is a common ailment. In time, it goes away. Unless it proves fatal."

Passing through the outskirts of Ch'ang-an, Prince Jen was appalled to observe the ramshackle dwellings, patched together with paper, straw, and plaster, none of them as spacious as the palace kennels or pigeon coops. Street urchins picked through heaps of rubbish, a bent-backed old woman and a dog lean as a skeleton disputed over a bone in the gutter.

"One of our nicer neighborhoods," Mafoo remarked.

"Can there be worse?" Jen burst out. "I never realized—Mafoo, I must learn all I can from Yuan-ming, and come back as soon as possible to help these folk."

"Agreed." Mafoo slapped the reins. "Especially the part about 'as soon as possible.' "

Passing the Happy Phoenix Gardens and crossing the Lotus Bridge, they left the capital well behind them. Prince Jen's earnest concern for what he had seen strengthened his resolution. At the same time, he could not imagine a pleasanter way to accomplish a noble purpose. Halting at the end of their first day on the road, Mafoo pitched a silk tent and set up comfortable couches; from the supply wagons, he obtained chairs, taborets, flowered screens, and a cooking brazier.

As courtesy required, Prince Jen invited Li Kwang to share the excellent meal Mafoo himself had prepared. After the obligatory expressions of gratitude, the gray-headed, battle-scarred warrior addressed Prince Jen.

"His Divine Majesty entrusted your life to my care," Li Kwang said. "I gave him my solemn vow that I and my men would guard you with our lives. Young Lord Prince, I repeat that vow to you."

"Honorable Li Kwang," Prince Jen graciously replied, "between you and my good servant, what harm can come to me?"

Next day, Prince Jen wondered if he had spoken too soon. The royal retinue had been following the River Lan, which Li Kwang intended crossing, thus gaining the easier roads through the western province. A disturbance at the head of the column caused Mafoo to rein in the horses. Moments later, Li Kwang galloped up, dripping wet.

"My outriders saw an old man struggling in the river," he reported. "They halted to pull him out."

"They did well," Prince Jen said. "Aiding the elderly is, as Master Hu taught me, one of the Fourteen Excellent Deeds."

"They failed," Li Kwang replied. "For all their efforts, my men could not remove him." Li Kwang added that he himself had plunged into the river and failed equally. Even at this moment, the hapless victim still struggled, his strength ebbing.

Puzzled as to why a simple matter had proved so difficult, Prince Jen impatiently jumped from the carriage and beckoned Mafoo to accompany him. At the banks of the Lan, he hurried down the grassy slope. Half a dozen of Li Kwang's soldiers continued striving vainly to haul ashore a frail, white-bearded figure. Prince Jen quickly realized that the soldiers were hindered by their armor and the quilted skirts of their tunics.

"Mafoo," Prince Jen ordered, "go yourself and pull him out."

Casting an uneasy eye at the swift current, Mafoo scrambled down to seize the old man by the scruff of the neck. Soon, however, Mafoo stumbled back to the side of Prince Jen.

"He's slippery as an eel!" Mafoo cried. "I can't keep hold of him. I must believe he prefers not to be rescued."

"Then why is he shouting for help?" Surprised at the inability of Mafoo, and seeing that no further moments could be wasted, Prince Jen strode to the water's edge. There, the aged man sputtered and blubbered, desperately begging for someone to save him.

Prince Jen rolled up the sleeves of his robe and took

a firm grip on the skinny hand reaching out to him. Next moment, Prince Jen's arm was clutched with astonishing vigor. Before he could dig in his heels, he found himself pulled headlong into the stream, seized around the neck, and so buffeted by flailing legs that he went spinning and choking to the riverbed.

* * * * *

Prince Jen's praiseworthy attempt has only put him in danger of being drowned. The outcome is told in the next chapter.

3

· Prince Jen's patience is severely tried ·
· A meddlesome passenger ·
· A muddy road ·

PRINCE JEN HAD NEVER IMAGINED anyone would be so stubborn about being rescued. Thrashing around in panic, the victim grappled with his would-be benefactor, and his struggles only hindered Prince Jen's efforts to save him. Mafoo and Li Kwang, seeing their master vanish below the surface, were after him instantly. By the time Prince Jen succeeded in getting a firm hold on the old man and bringing him to the water's edge, servant and warrior were on hand to haul him ashore. The object of Prince Jen's good deed at last released his grip and fell in a heap on the grassy slope.

"Young Lord," said Li Kwang, "I beg you: Never again put your noble person at such risk."

"Being helpful is one thing," Mafoo added. "Getting drowned is something else."

Prince Jen had no breath to answer. His robes were sopping, the tide had carried off his gold cap, and he felt that he had swallowed a good portion of the Lan. He gratefully allowed Mafoo to peel away the duckweed entwining him.

As for the old man, strings of white hair clung to his half-bald cranium and his robe had dredged up mud from the river bottom, but he seemed no worse for his harrowing experience. He shook himself like a wet dog, scuttled over, and knocked his head at the Young Lord's feet, showering him with gratitude and water. It took a few moments for Prince Jen to realize that Master Fu, as he identified himself, had addressed him by name.

"You and your most excellent and honorable mission are everywhere known," Master Fu replied when Prince Jen asked how he had been recognized. Master Fu explained further, without being asked, that he was a poor wandering scholar, that he had been so absorbed in a treatise on how to travel safely that he had paid more attention to his reading than to his feet and had unwittingly strayed from his path.

"All has ended well," Prince Jen said, impatient to get into dry clothing and set off again. "Go your way safely."

Master Fu clasped his hands. "Young Lord, my poor

strength is gone. Allow me a little while to regain it. Let me ride with your escort, only a short distance along the road. It would be one of the Eighty-seven Acts of Kindness."

"There should be an eighty-eighth," put in Mafoo, cocking a sharp eye at the scholar. "Don't impose on someone's good nature."

Master Fu clapped a hand to his brow. "Forgive me, Young Lord. How did I dare—what could I have been thinking of? I should never dream of delaying you by so much as an instant. What possessed me? To save my wretched self a few steps? No, no, better I should perish ignominiously, shrivel up like a husk on the highway, rather than put Your Lordship to even a moment of inconvenience. Ten thousand blessings on you for saving my ignoble, despicable existence—no matter what becomes of it later."

Master Fu picked up the staff he had dropped in the process of falling into the river. Snuffling, moaning, holding first his head, then the small of his back, he tottered away.

"Wait." Prince Jen beckoned him. "Ride with my escort. Go and find yourself a place."

The old scholar burst out with another ten thousand blessings and made his way up the bank with more agility than he had shown before.

"For the sake of mercy, what else could I have done?" Prince Jen asked Mafoo, who had come back with dry clothing. "Pitiful creature, I had no heart to deny him. A modest favor—"

"Which he accepted nimbly enough," Mafoo said as they hurried back to the roadside. There, Prince Jen found Master Fu sprawled comfortably in the carriage.

"Forgive me once more," Master Fu said. "I only wished to rest my aching bones before submitting them to the jolting of the baggage cart, the proper place for this unworthy individual. I shall remove my humble self from your radiant presence, even though I am so weak from hunger my head is spinning. Absorbed in study, I forgot to eat. My sack of food is nourishing the fish in the Lan. No matter, I shall scrape something from a refuse pit and hope to keep body and soul together."

Master Fu looked so woebegone and truly so close to starvation that Prince Jen ordered Mafoo to fetch food and drink.

"Only a sip of water," Master Fu insisted. "A handful of millet. Unless there might be a few drops of stale beer. Or a tiny morsel of carp. And if, in your compassionate generosity, you saw fit to add a chicken wing—"

Mafoo, at Prince Jen's instruction, brought back victuals from the kitchen wagon. By the time the escort set off again, Master Fu, protesting all the while, had downed four pots of beer, two fish, and a whole chicken, along with eight rice cakes. His ability to consume large quantities of food was matched only by his endless chatter. Belching loudly, scratching himself, dripping water over the upholstery, Master Fu never stopped talking. From the moment the procession began

ay along the road, he rambled on about
gical theories, mixing them in the same
with complaints about his bunions, his poor di-
stion, and the palpitations of his liver.

Master Fu suddenly broke off his catalog of ailments
and stared around him. "But—but we travel in the
wrong direction," he cried. "We are going west!"

"Indeed so," Mafoo replied.

Master Fu's jaw dropped. "Did I neglect to mention
that my path lies eastward?"

"Tiresome old crock!" exclaimed Mafoo, whose patience had been shrinking with each moment in the
scholar's company. "You should have spoken up
sooner."

Master Fu turned to Prince Jen. "I have only myself
to blame. Through no fault of your own, your
munificent kindness has put me in a worse state than
before. However, it is the intention, not the result, that
gains you merit. No matter that my toes are swollen,
my knees trembling. Set me down here, I shall retrace
the steps your benevolence made me lose."

"Excellent idea," said Mafoo.

"Leave him on the road?" Prince Jen said. "I meant
to do him a small kindness, not a great disservice. We
will take him where he wishes."

Prince Jen ordered the retinue to turn east. The
grateful Master Fu assured him that the delay would be
no more than half an hour's time. Yet, whenever Prince
Jen suggested they had gone far enough, Master Fu
begged him to keep on a few moments longer.

Throughout, Master Fu never left off his constant chatter. And, despite his accidental bath in the Lan, he generated an assortment of odors as distressing as they were various.

"This Master Fu is a pitiful, needy creature," Jen told himself. "Surely, he deserves assistance. Even so, it would have been pleasanter to do a kindness for someone who talked a little less and smelled a little better."

Master Hu would have judged this thought as uncharitable, so Jen made every effort to tolerate the old scholar. This grew more difficult, for Master Fu proved to be as meddlesome as a monkey. He examined the appointments of the carriage, fingered the upholstery, and peered under the seats. His eyes inevitably fell on the silk-wrapped gifts. Before Prince Jen could stop him, Master Fu seized upon them. He pulled away the covering from the saddle and studied it inquisitively.

"It is not my lowly place to question the Young Lord," Master Fu said, "but would this be a gift for Yuan-ming? It is a handsome saddle. Yet, allow me to make a humble observation. It puzzles me that the great Yuan-ming should be offered something less than perfect. See here, the cinch belt is broken and has come loose. If Yuan-ming were to use this gift, he might suffer a serious, even fatal, fall."

Prince Jen was equally puzzled. As far as he knew, the saddle had been undamaged when they had left Ch'ang-an. Now, clearly, the cinch was broken. As he wondered about this, Li Kwang rode up.

"It is not practical for us to go farther," he said,

gesturing toward brambles and dense shrubbery. Only the narrowest of lanes led where Master Fu had begged to be taken. "Even my foot soldiers would have difficulty following such a path, and many more hours of delay."

"The difficulty isn't the path, it's the passenger," Mafoo told Prince Jen. "Enough is enough. You saved his life, filled his belly, put up with his yammering, and eased his journey past anything that ancient crackpot could expect. We have two choices: Take him by the scruff of the neck and throw him out, or take him by the seat of his pants and throw him out."

"I shall burden you no more," put in Master Fu. "I am so close to my destination, barely another half hour. Let me go now on my poor, tottering legs. What difference if my weak old heart fails me and I die in the bushes? Young Lord, with my last breath I shall bless you for your kind intention."

With Master Fu wheezing, moaning, and already going blue in the face, Prince Jen could not bring himself to follow Mafoo's advice. "We've carried him this far," he said to Li Kwang. "It would shame me not to go the rest of such a little way. The lane is wide enough for my carriage. Mafoo and I shall drive him where he wishes. You and your men wait here."

Li Kwang, uncomfortable at letting his prince out of his sight, offered to ride with him.

"There is no need," Prince Jen said. "I would rather you attend to another task." He showed Li Kwang the damaged saddle. "Have one of your men repair this."

Li Kwang examined the saddle. "It is easily mended. The leather is not broken, it has merely come loose. I myself will see to it, and have it ready by the time you return."

Mafoo, grumbling, turned the carriage into the rutted lane. "The only good part of this," he muttered, "is that we'll soon be rid of the old geezer once and for all."

The lane, however, became rougher and rougher. Despite Mafoo's capable hands on the reins, the horses could barely make their way. Lurching and jolting, the carriage went at a snail's pace. Master Fu kept insisting that his destination, the village of Kwan-tzu, lay only moments away.

Two hours had already passed when, as if out of sheer spitefulness, the bright sky suddenly clouded. Rain bucketed down in such blinding sheets that Mafoo could only let the horses stumble ahead at their own slow gait.

The lane, difficult enough to begin with, turned quickly into a river of mud. The horses nearly foundered; the carriage slewed from side to side and, with a bone-shattering jolt, stopped altogether. Mafoo shouted and slapped the reins, the horses strained, but the wheels only sank deeper in the mire.

Cursing under his breath, Mafoo climbed down and put his shoulder to one of the rear wheels, hoping to dislodge it. As the work proved too hard for him alone, he ordered Master Fu to lend a hand and make himself useful.

"Gladly," Master Fu replied. "No matter that the weather has touched off my rheumatism."

"Then hold the reins." Prince Jen, frankly wishing he had never laid eyes on the scholar, sprang from the carriage to join Mafoo.

While Master Fu, sitting dry and comfortable under the canopy, called out words of encouragement, Prince Jen and Mafoo hauled and heaved as best they could. The rain fell harder and the mud deepened.

"Give it up," Mafoo panted. "We're stuck. There's only one thing to do."

◆ ◆ ◆ ◆ ◆

Having already been over his head in water, our hero is up to his ears in mud, a situation hardly befitting his rank. What happens next is told in the following chapter.

4

· *The yamen of Cha-wei* ·
· *Voyaging Moon solves one problem* ·
· *Another arises* ·

"I SUGGEST THE FOLLOWING," Mafoo said. "I take one of Master Fu's ankles. You take the other. Then we turn him upside down and stick his miserable head in this mud as deep as we can."

"How will that move the carriage?" Prince Jen said.

"It won't," Mafoo said, "but it will cheer me up considerably."

"Why blame him?" Prince Jen said, bending all his strength against the sunken wheel. "None of this is his fault."

"Isn't it?" Mafoo retorted. "If he hadn't fallen into the river, you wouldn't have pulled him out. If you hadn't pulled him out, he wouldn't have begged a ride. If he hadn't begged a ride, we wouldn't have gone out of our way. If we hadn't gone out of our way, we wouldn't be wallowing in muck up to our ears."

Prince Jen gritted his teeth. Contrary to the instructions of Master Hu concerning respect for the elderly and the Eighty-seven Acts of Kindness, at this moment he would have been delighted to follow Mafoo's suggestion. His fingers itched to seize Master Fu not by the ankles but by the exasperating wretch's skinny neck. Instead, he flung himself against the wheel and strained and heaved beside Mafoo.

The carriage moved, rolled back a little, and finally lurched free. Mafoo's shout of triumph turned to a groan of dismay.

"We're no better off," he cried. "Look here. Half the spokes are cracked. The wheel won't hold." Hands on hips, he glumly regarded the disabled vehicle. "We have two choices. We can unhitch both horses and ride back to the main road. Or I take one horse, and you stay in the carriage and wait until Li Kwang sends help."

"What is the difficulty?" Master Fu had climbed onto the backseat, where he had been observing with great interest the efforts of Prince Jen and Mafoo. "The wheel will hold for a little distance. In Kwan-tzu, it can be repaired while you find shelter. Only a few moments more."

Prince Jen hesitated. As the rain pelted down, apart from throttling Master Fu, the one thing he most wished for was a roof over his head. Wet and exhausted, he would have been grateful for the roughest comfort.

"One instant longer than those few moments," he said, "and you will have a heavy account to settle with me."

"Allow me to disagree," Mafoo said. "I'll be the one to settle his account."

Master Fu, for once, proved accurate in his claims. The wheel wobbled but did not break. As twilight gathered, Prince Jen saw lights glowing ahead, sooner even than Master Fu promised. An added relief, the downpour stopped as suddenly as it had begun.

Entering the village of Kwan-tzu, Mafoo trotted the horses across a little public square, its ground dry and hard-packed, as if there had never been a rainstorm. He had no need to ask the location of the yamen. The headquarters of the local official was the biggest building in Kwan-tzu, surrounded by high walls, the only entry an iron gate.

The watchman's jaw dropped in astonishment when Mafoo announced the arrival of the Young Lord Prince. He hurried to fling open the gate and call for attendants to receive the royal visitor. Within moments, a handful of bewildered servants came scrambling out, stunned and mystified by Jen's presence in the village. Mafoo drove the carriage into the courtyard. Stepping down, Prince Jen glanced over his shoulder. He saw nothing of the old scholar. Master Fu, for reasons of his own, must have clambered from the other side of the vehicle and scurried off into one of the alleys. Prince Jen heaved a thankful sigh, not in any way unhappy over Master Fu's disappearance without a word of gratitude.

The village administrator now came forward. Cha-wei by name, this Official of the Third Rank looked as mystified as his servants.

"Young Lord Prince! What a joyful surprise!" Cha-wei bowed and made every effort to twist his long-jawed face into an expression of pleasure. "Still more amazing, you are unharmed. Ferocious bandits—the Yellow Scarves—have been attacking all travelers in these parts. How did you escape such danger?"

"I saw no bandits," Jen replied. "The only dangers were being soaked to the skin by the rainstorm and my carriage foundering in the mud. A wheel is damaged. Have it repaired. Meantime, I and my servant will change into dry clothing."

"Yes, yes, Young Lord, as you command. Only forgive me for not offering hospitality at once." Cha-wei wrung his hands and blinked his close-set eyes. "My astonishment, my relief at your safety, made me forget proper courtesy. Alas, this wretched yamen is ill-prepared to offer a fitting welcome. Even so, I beg you to avail yourself of my humble and most unworthy facilities."

"They will be sufficient for our needs," Prince Jen

replied. "See to my carriage immediately. I wish to leave as soon as possible."

"Your visitation will be short? I am filled with unbearably painful regret," returned Cha-wei, brightening. He clapped his hands, ordering attendants to conduct Prince Jen and Mafoo to the best available chambers.

"Hardly the Celestial Palace," observed Mafoo, after servants had brought fresh robes, "but not too bad for the provinces. I'd guess that Cha-wei treats himself well enough. What official doesn't?"

Mafoo was correct, as Prince Jen discovered when they were led to Cha-wei's private apartments. There, tables had been spread with quite acceptable refreshments. In addition, Cha-wei had summoned his household musicians. With the melodies of zither and flute, the chiming of bells, the tuneful sounds mixing with incense from iron braziers, Prince Jen felt reasonably at ease for the first time in a trying day. He briefly explained the events that had brought him to the village.

Cha-wei gave him a puzzled look. "How interesting that Your Lordship mentions a downpour. Highly localized atmospheric disturbances, of course, are not impossible. Nevertheless, here we have not had a drop of rain for five days."

"You saw our clothing," Jen curtly replied, "wet and muddy. Honorable Cha-wei, I know when I've been rained on."

Cha-wei tactfully let the matter drop and begged his royal guest to speak more of the purpose of his journey. Prince Jen's fatigue, however, must have weighed on him more heavily than he realized, for he found his thoughts drifting away, floating with the music, soaring with the shimmering tones of the flute. Only when Mafoo nudged him did he abruptly raise his head and open his eyes.

"Whatever Your Lordship requires . . ." Cha-wei was saying.

"Oh? Yes—" Prince Jen blinked. He had, for the moment, been happily elsewhere. The voice of the flute had led him spinning like a leaf in a silver stream, past waterfalls that turned into rainbows and rainbows that turned into bright-plumaged birds. Cha-wei's yamen was a dull, boring place in comparison.

"What His Lordship requires," put in Mafoo helpfully, seeing his master look around absently, "is an armed escort. With dangerous bandits in the vicinity, the Young Lord must not travel unguarded."

"Mafoo is right," Prince Jen said. "Yes, we wish an escort. Assemble them, have them ready with their weapons. A dozen mounted men should suffice."

"It should, if only I had them to offer," Cha-wei replied. "Lord Prince, I beg your gracious indulgence. There is not one able-bodied man in Kwan-tzu. They are all in the countryside, seeking to capture the bandits."

"The Young Lord must have a suitable escort nonetheless," Mafoo said. "Lacking anyone else, that leaves yourself and your attendants."

"That would be an honor beyond what I deserve," replied Cha-wei. "My servants—mere cooks, clerks, low-ranking deputies and their assistants—are entirely unworthy of such a noble task."

"Then," demanded Mafoo, "what do you suggest?"

"Ah—yes, what I suggest," Cha-wei answered, "is another joyful possibility." Cha-wei looked as if he had swallowed a bowl of scalding tea as he continued. "I urge His Lordship to accept my hospitality, wretched and despicable though it is, for a week, ten days perhaps, until the village men return."

"I cannot be delayed that long," said Prince Jen.

"Out of the question," agreed Mafoo. "There's nothing else for it," he added, as Cha-wei's features grew more and more pained, "you and your servants will have to do. So, put on your armor if you have any. You'll need swords, lances, bows and arrows."

"What bliss," Cha-wei murmured in a strangled voice, "to die in the service of the Young Lord."

"If His Lordship permits me to address him, I know a better way."

These words came from one of the musicians, a girl who set aside her flute and came forward to approach Prince Jen.

"Forgive such impertinence," Cha-wei hastily put in. "This pitiful creature is Voyaging Moon, a bond-maid who has shown some small ability in music. I have taken a slight degree of—of benign interest in her well-being. Ignorant, ill-favored though she is, her thoughts might conceivably be of value. Your Lordship may deign to favor her by listening to them."

"Let her speak," said Prince Jen. Until now, he had taken little notice of the individual musicians. The flute girl, however, had caught his full attention. Compared with the noble ladies in the Celestial Palace, Voyaging Moon could hardly count as beautiful. Far from an oval perfection, her face had the sharp, high cheekbones of eastern province peasants. Instead of being arranged in a lacquered tower, the girl's black hair hung loose over her shoulders and was held only by a white headband. He motioned for her to continue.

"An armed escort might offer some protection," Voyaging Moon said in a voice that Jen found as melodious as her instrument. "At the same time, it would attract unwanted attention. These bandits will stop at nothing. Their leader calls himself Natha Yellow Scarf. He's worse than the rest of them put together. He'd be more than happy to cut your throat. So, the best thing would be to go quickly, quietly, and not be seen at all."

"Exactly as I was about to say," exclaimed Cha-wei. "Much as I yearn to give my life defending the Young Lord, I reluctantly admit that her idea has merit."

"In other words, I'm to travel secretly? Furtively?" said Prince Jen. "Do you think it honorable for me to skulk like a coward through my own kingdom?"

"I'd have supposed that skulking was part of a princely education," Voyaging Moon said.

"Certainly not," retorted Jen.

"Then here's a chance to learn," said Voyaging Moon.

"She's right," Mafoo whispered. "Better to be unnoticed than dead. A little skulking never harmed anyone."

"I was born and raised in this district," the girl continued. "I know pathways that will keep you clear of Natha and his gang. They'll never catch a glimpse of you. Now, I can see Your Lordship's about to suggest taking me as a guide. A brilliant idea. For my ignoble self, it would be the honor of a lifetime, enshrined forever in my memory. Naturally, my esteemed master would have to agree to do without my worthless presence for a short time."

"Oh, I agree, I agree," burst out Cha-wei.

"Yes, well then—" Jen began. The girl was looking straight at him. She had used all the proper terms of self-deprecation, but he had the uneasy feeling she meant not a word of them. "Now that you've suggested—or I was going to suggest," he stammered, "your presence with us would be a pleasure. That is, useful. Very acceptable."

Cha-wei, sighing with happy relief, eagerly offered to provide a horse on which the flute girl could return to the village. It was decided that all would be ready by daybreak, and Prince Jen and Mafoo were again installed in their sleeping chamber.

"About that flute girl," Jen said as he stretched on the couch, "I'm glad for her help. But—did you find her somehow irreverent? Impertinent, even?"

"No more than I am." Mafoo yawned. "You'll manage to put up with her."

Prince Jen did not reply, and soon fell asleep. But the voice of the flute echoed in his ears. The features of the girl filled his dreams. He awoke feeling vaguely unsettled and too distracted to observe and properly admire the rising sun.

The artisans had repaired the wheel. The girl, in coarse cotton trousers and jacket, waited at the carriage. Because of her knowledge of the countryside, Mafoo allowed her to take the reins. Cha-wei, at the yamen gate, did his best to look heartbroken by the early departure of his royal guest.

Prince Jen would gladly have conversed with the flute girl, but each time he tried, he grew strangely tongue-tied. At last, he gave up his attempts. His glances, nevertheless, continually went to Voyaging Moon.

For her part, the girl was as good as her word. She followed practically invisible paths and trails, driving quickly and efficiently. Prince Jen, in fact, felt a twinge of regret at reaching the road so soon.

His regret turned to alarm when Voyaging Moon drew up at the spot where he had left his escort. He sprang from the carriage. Looking in every direction, he saw nothing of Li Kwang or a single one of his men. The road lay empty.

* * * * *

Has our hero begun to develop some affection for a flute girl? A more urgent question: What has become of Li Kwang and his warriors? The answer is given in the next chapter.

5

· *The Tale of the Warrior's Saddle* ·

HONORABLE GENERAL LI KWANG had never lacked in courage or failed in duty. Among themselves, his men called him "Broken Face" because of all the battle scars crisscrossing his cheeks and brow. They were devoted to him, though, and would have followed him to the ends of the earth.

Now, on this journey to T'ien-kuo, Li Kwang had vowed to guard his prince with his life. Uncomfortable at the Young Lord's decision to part from his escort even for an hour, Li Kwang watched, frowning, as the carriage turned off into the narrow lane. Li Kwang thought, first, of galloping after him; but Prince Jen had ordered Li Kwang to wait, and so he did.

Telling himself that his unease was groundless, that no harm could befall the prince in such a brief period of time, Li Kwang ordered his men to stand to their arms while he turned his attention to the saddle he had undertaken to mend.

As he worked, Li Kwang marveled at the craftsmanship given to the making of the saddle. Intricate patterns had been tooled into the leather, itself soft and smooth as silk. The stirrups and the bit were of burnished gold.

"This truly is a gift fit for a king," Li Kwang said. "Never have I seen anything to match it."

Most astonishing to Li Kwang, however, was not its excellence but its lightness. Finishing his task easily and quickly, he now found the saddle and all its harness weighed next to nothing.

"No more than a butterfly!" he exclaimed. "Less than a feather!"

The more he marveled, the more he yearned to try it out for himself.

"Such a saddle will never again come into my hands," Li Kwang thought. "Still, it would be improper for me to use what is meant as an offering to a mighty monarch."

While he stood, chin in hand, admiring the saddle, his roan mare, Autumn Dew, trotted to his side. She was the most faithful and obedient of steeds, answering to Li Kwang's lightest touch on the reins, to his smallest gesture or softest word of command.

"And you," said Li Kwang, stroking her high-arching neck, "you have long gone heavily burdened and carried me, my weapons, and my armor without complaint. Would it not be a pleasure for you to feel the comfort of such a fine harness?"

Autumn Dew nuzzled the saddle, then whickered and tossed her head.

"You admire it as much as I do," Li Kwang said, smiling wistfully, "but it is destined for the great Yuan-ming, and too magnificent for any of lower station."

About to put it carefully aside, Li Kwang hesitated a moment.

"This is a piece of ancient workmanship," he said. "Who made it and for whom, I do not know. But, in all those years, many must have ridden on it, and they could not have been every one a king. What difference could one more rider make?"

Nevertheless, he told himself that as long as it was in his charge he would not meddle with it. Still, he could not keep from running a hand over the saddle, which grew more beautiful the more he looked at it.

"Once given to Yuan-ming, what then?" Li Kwang said. "No doubt it will be locked in his treasure house. Yuan-ming may well have a dozen others more splendid than this, and it would mean nothing to him. What a waste if it were merely stored away to gather dust."

But that, Li Kwang told himself, did not concern him. What Yuan-ming chose to do with the gift was a matter for the king's own judgment.

He turned away, hoping that Prince Jen would soon come back so they could set off again and Li Kwang could rid his mind of tempting thoughts.

"One thing troubles me," Li Kwang said. "Suppose Yuan-ming does not store it away but makes use of it. How can I be sure it is well mended? How do I know the repairs will hold?

"Suppose, for example," Li Kwang went on, "Yuan-ming rides to the hunt. What if the saddle gives way and he falls? If he falls, he might break a limb, or even be killed. That would be my fault."

Satisfied that he understood his responsibility and obligation, he unharnessed Autumn Dew and replaced her saddle with the gift for Yuan-ming. The mare pranced and curvetted with pleasure, and it gladdened Li Kwang's heart to see how handsome his beloved steed looked. All the harness leathers seemed firmly in place.

"Even so," Li Kwang said, "nothing is proved without practice. If there is any risk, I must be the one to take it. I must seat myself and ride a few moments. Only then will I be certain. That is my duty. Afterward, I will put it away and explain to Prince Jen what I did, and why, and how thoroughly I completed my task."

Hesitating no longer, Li Kwang mounted. No sooner was he astride than Autumn Dew reared, whin-

nied, and shook her mane. Then she laid back her ears
and bolted like an arrow down the road. The startled
Li Kwang pulled back on the reins. The usually obedient Autumn Dew only stretched into a faster gallop.

Li Kwang was a skilled horseman, but he could do
nothing to curb Autumn Dew. He called out to her,
coaxing with every endearment, soothing, commanding,
all in vain. He thought, then, to risk leaping from her
back. He could not kick his feet free of the stirrups or
lift himself out of the saddle. He waved his arms and
shouted for his men to help.

Li Kwang's cavalry troopers, seeing their commander's gestures, believed he was ordering them to
follow. They leaped astride their horses and galloped
after him. The foot soldiers likewise misunderstood.
They seized their weapons and set off running as fast as
their legs could carry them to catch up with their comrades. The drivers of the baggage carts and supply wagons whipped up their animals. In moments, all the train
of warriors and retainers was streaming down the
road. The wagoners caught their breath in astonishment
at the speed of their usually slow-paced horses. The
pack mules sped over the ground as if their burdens
weighed nothing. The foot soldiers found themselves
racing without effort, their boots barely skimming the
road.

The wind whistled in Li Kwang's ears as Autumn
Dew galloped ever more swiftly. After a little while,
the mare veered sharply eastward off the road and

plunged into the undergrowth. Twisted branches sprang out at Li Kwang. He flung up his arms, expecting to be swept from Autumn Dew's back. Suddenly the branches drew aside, the brambles and bushes opened before him, the undergrowth parted, and a clear pathway rose toward high mountains ahead.

Li Kwang glanced back. Behind him, his warriors never slackened their pace. Still they climbed, higher and higher. The time must have sped as quickly as Autumn Dew, for Li Kwang grew aware of the sun setting—or so he supposed, for the mountaintops, gray and bare, blazed red as rubies.

Autumn Dew galloped on. The mare made straight for a rocky mass towering above the neighboring peaks. At the foot of the mountain, she still kept her wild course. Li Kwang saw the black mouth of a cavern. Autumn Dew sped into it.

Here, Li Kwang was sure she must halt. A wall of stone rose just ahead. At the approach of Autumn Dew, it split in two and the huge slabs of stone fell open. Li Kwang was borne past these massive portals into the mountain's heart.

His men followed, riders and foot soldiers alike. Once they had entered, Li Kwang heard an earthshaking rumble as the giant slabs swung shut behind him and all his troops.

Li Kwang was a brave warrior, but seeing himself and his men so trapped, his courage almost faltered. Autumn Dew trotted on, picking her way delicately over loose stones rattling beneath her hooves. Li Kwang could see nothing in the darkness that had swallowed him. He dropped the reins and let Autumn Dew go where she pleased. The mare, unhesitating, continued down long galleries and corridors.

A burst of light dazzled Li Kwang. Autumn Dew, he thought as his heart leaped, had found a passage outward. When his vision cleared, he knew he was still deep within the mountain. He rubbed his eyes but still did not believe them. Stretching to a horizon wide as the world spread rich green fields, woodlands, and terraces. Rivers and streams sparkled under a cloudless sky. As he looked, his amazement gave way to a sense of peace and harmony. Li Kwang's delight grew as the mare carried him down a well-paved street into a large town.

Here, he saw busy marketplaces, open-fronted shops, weavers at their looms, potters at their wheels, passersby, men and women in bright costumes, children at their games. At the sight of the train of warriors, the townsfolk ran to wave and smile, as if Li Kwang and his men had been long awaited.

There now approached Li Kwang a tall woman clad in robes of silver spun as fine as silk. Long silver tresses fell from beneath a headdress set with every kind of precious gem. Li Kwang at last found himself able to swing down from the saddle as the woman drew closer.

"I am the Lady of Fearful Awakenings," she said, making a graceful gesture of welcome. Smiling, she gazed at him with eyes the color of burnished copper. "And you are the one called 'Broken Face Kwang.' "

"How do you know this?" Li Kwang murmured. "Where have I come?"

"Where you have often wished to be."

She beckoned for him to accompany her, indicating an unwalled building a little distance ahead. The structure was more palatial than Li Kwang had ever seen, with high-peaked, sharply curved roofs set one on top of the other, tall towers, and ornamental bridges. All around were gardens filled with blossoms and orchards laden with golden fruit. Li Kwang heard bird songs and the chiming of wind bells.

Li Kwang held back for a moment. "What of my men and horses? And my own steed, Autumn Dew? We have ridden hard and far."

"They will be as well attended as yourself."

The Lady of Fearful Awakenings spoke so reassuringly that Li Kwang went happily with her. As they walked side by side, hand in hand, Li Kwang gathered from her words that she already knew of Prince Jen's journey and its purpose and the happenings that had brought Li Kwang into the mountain. How was this possible, wondered Li Kwang, and why should one so beautiful be so unfortunately named?

These questions vanished from his mind as the Lady of Fearful Awakenings led him up a broad flight of steps and into a spacious chamber. The ceilings rose so high that he could not see where they ended. Shafts of

sunlight filled the room and the hallways beyond. Yet
he barely glanced at the handsome furnishings, for a
heavy weariness had come to settle over him. His eyes
began closing despite himself, his legs felt leaden, and
he gladly allowed the Lady of Fearful Awakenings to
draw him to a couch that seemed in readiness for him.

"Rest a while," the Lady of Fearful Awakenings
said as Li Kwang sank into the deep cushions. She covered his face with her hands. Li Kwang gratefully
closed his eyes.

The fatigue that overwhelmed him did not come
entirely from his ride through the countryside. It was,
rather, as if all battles he had ever fought now pressed
upon him. Every step marched, every league ridden
compressed into a single massive burden.

For a time, he dreamed of those past combats, of
hissing arrows, bloody swords, riders clashing, horses
shrieking and striking out with their hooves. Cries of
the wounded and dying filled his ears, the reek of old
battlefields choked his nostrils.

The nightmares faded. In their place arose mineral
visions: sharp-edged stars of crystals, geometric shapes
shifting and combining, growing like frost patterns;
mountains cleaved to reveal dark inner veins; snow-
flakes of garnet; the dreams a stone might dream.

He awoke. The chamber had vanished.

Li Kwang sat astride Autumn Dew. They were in
the cavern once again. Unable to move arms or legs, he
could open his eyes no more than a crack. Crystalline

growths jutted like fangs around him and gave a dim greenish glow. Glancing down with difficulty, as if his eyes had frozen in their sockets, he glimpsed his hands on the reins. A cry like rocks grinding together caught in his throat.

Li Kwang had turned to stone.

So had Autumn Dew. Li Kwang could not see them, but knew with cold certainty that his warriors shared the same fate.

He tried to fathom how this had come about, hoping that by doing so he might devise a way to free his warriors from this horrible captivity. But his thoughts moved as slowly as a glacier. Time itself seemed turned to stone—he could not calculate how long he had slept or how long he had been in the cavern. He only understood how well named had been the Lady of Fearful Awakenings.

Despite all, deep within his shell of stone he sensed a constant throbbing, and he envisioned a crimson spark pulsing faintly but steadily. As long as his heart beat, he knew himself to be a living man.

A tall form took shape in front of him. Li Kwang's eyes had become crystal prisms and he saw a dozen images of an old man in a red robe.

"I have been waiting for you," Master Wu said. "You have slept, now you must wake."

"You? Here?" murmured Li Kwang. "Was it you who caused this?"

"I cause nothing," Master Wu replied, "though

from time to time I make arrangements. Had you not tried the saddle, things would have gone otherwise. Now, they are what they are and what they must be. You are in Wu-shan, Mountain of Sorcerers."

"What of Prince Jen?" Li Kwang said. "If I failed him, if I did not guard him as I vowed, let me not fail him again. How can I rejoin him?"

"Prince Jen follows his own road," Master Wu said, "and must go wherever it may lead him. Your path has taken a different turning."

"I accept my punishment," Li Kwang said. "The blame is mine alone. Therefore, I ask you to free my warriors. They followed me, but this was their duty, not their fault. I ask you as well to free Autumn Dew. Her place is not here. Allow her, at least, to return to the fields and forests and the open sky."

"Broken Face Kwang," Master Wu said, "your words do you credit. You will gain merit for them. Whatever else," he added with half a smile, "you do not have a heart of stone.

"I cannot grant your wish entirely," Master Wu continued. "That is not in my power, but in yours."

"How?" Li Kwang replied. "I can no more move from this spot than could a rock or a boulder."

"Have you the will to do it?" Master Wu said. "Try."

Summoning all his strength of spirit, Li Kwang discovered that indeed he could move a little, and Autumn Dew likewise; but so grindingly and agonizingly that all effort seemed doomed to fail. Nevertheless, whatever the painful cost, he resolved to guide his faithful horse and warriors into the sunlit world of living beings.

Master Wu nodded, satisfied by Li Kwang's determination, and gave him certain instructions. "Only if you are able to follow them," he added, "only then can there be any shred of hope."

"Given that much," Li Kwang said, "I ask no more."

* * * * *

Leaving Li Kwang and his stone warriors to whatever the future holds for them, we now return to Prince Jen, Voyaging Moon, and Mafoo. How they deal with their own plight is told in the following chapter.

6

THE ONLY TRACE OF THE WARRIORS was a saddle by the roadside. Prince Jen knelt to examine it.

"This is Li Kwang's." He glanced anxiously at Mafoo. "Where is the one I gave him to mend?"

"Forgive this unspeakably ignorant flute girl for even daring to say this," put in Voyaging Moon, "but when all of your people seem to have disappeared, and you're far from your palace, alone in the middle of nowhere, very likely without provisions, one saddle more or less is the least of your worries."

"The least?" Prince Jen cried. "It was in my charge. A gift for Yuan-ming. Master Wu chose it." He stammered out a quick account of his journey and its purpose.

"I understand why you'd want it back," Voyaging Moon said. "Of course, you've already considered the possibility that your officer left his own saddle here and put the other on his horse."

"He could have," Prince Jen said. "But why? And why isn't he here? He was ordered to wait for me."

"First, find him," Voyaging Moon said, "then you'll find what happened."

"Oh, brilliant!" Mafoo snorted. "And how to do that?"

"But surely you know." Voyaging Moon smiled at Mafoo. "By now, you've looked at the roadway. And very cleverly observed the hoofprints and wagon tracks."

"Eh?" said Mafoo. "Oh. Yes, I was just about to do that."

"Not that a shrewd, quick-witted fellow like you needs any help," Voyaging Moon added, "but if I were asked, I might agree to come along. In case—a remote possibility, but just in case—you missed some tiny detail."

"There's a slight odor of rat somewhere in this," Mafoo murmured to Prince Jen. "She has something else in mind."

"Would you help us?" Prince Jen asked eagerly,

paying no attention to Mafoo. "Cha-wei will commend you for a good deed."

"I doubt it," Voyaging Moon said. "He won't have the chance. I'm not setting foot in Kwan-tzu again. I've run off."

"There's the rat!" cried Mafoo. "I knew I smelled one."

"The Honorable Cha-wei thinks I'm with you," Voyaging Moon said to Prince Jen. "By the time it occurs to him that I'm permanently missing, and he searches for me, I'll be out of reach. If he does happen to catch up with me—why, I'm simply doing the Young Lord a service."

"You left your master without permission?" said Prince Jen, taken aback. "You've committed a serious crime."

"I certainly have," Voyaging Moon happily agreed. "Cha-wei plans to bestow a great honor on me."

"Then why run away? You should be grateful."

"Do you think so?" said Voyaging Moon. "First, let me tell you this. My father was a peasant; he could barely feed himself, let alone a family. When my mother died, he sold me to a spice merchant in Kwan-tzu. The merchant raised me as a handmaiden for his wife. I was taught to read and write, play the flute, prepare tea correctly, and all such accomplishments. In time, the merchant wanted an important favor from Cha-wei. I was offered as a gift, which Cha-wei was pleased to accept. The merchant got his favor. Cha-wei got a flute girl.

"Now," she went on, "he wants to honor me by installing me in his bedchamber. That's an honor I decided to do without."

"I'm glad—I mean, that is, I can understand," Jen replied. "Yes, but—regrettably, the law is clear. It requires me to send you back immediately. I don't want to, but—"

"Young Lord," Mafoo whispered, drawing Jen aside, "just between the two of us, I'm not quite as clever as this flute girl thinks I am. Tracks? I can't even see them, let alone follow them. The law's already broken. What's the harm in breaking it a little more? In any case, you're the prince. The law's what you decide it is."

Prince Jen grinned. "As I was just about to say."

With Mafoo jogging behind in the carriage, Prince Jen tried to keep pace with the girl's long strides. After a time, Voyaging Moon halted and pointed toward the hills. From the torn undergrowth and trampled ground, she judged that the warriors had gone straight into the uplands. However, no sooner did Mafoo try to turn off the road than the mended wheel shattered again. The vehicle lurched and sent him tumbling into the bushes. Crawling out, shaking his fist, Mafoo laid this new misfortune on the head of Master Fu.

"We've had bad luck ever since we laid eyes on him!" cried Mafoo. "He plagues us even when he isn't here!"

"Leave the carriage, it's useless," Voyaging Moon

said. "We can bring the horses—as you were about to suggest."

Mafoo unhitched the animals. Prince Jen took the bundle of gifts. Having endangered, perhaps even lost, one of them, he chose to carry the rest himself. They pressed through the undergrowth, following the sure-footed Voyaging Moon. For well into the afternoon, they continued upward, walking their mounts where the woods grew too dense. A little before dusk, the girl halted at the foot of a towering mass of gray rock, dotted with patches of scrubby vegetation. The tracks led to the mouth of a cave.

"They've taken shelter there," Prince Jen said. He ran ahead into the cavern. He could see nothing in the deep shadows. He called out Li Kwang's name. Only echoes came back. Tethering the horses, Voyaging Moon and Mafoo brought in torches they had made from dead branches. The flickering light showed an earthen floor marked by boots and hooves.

"Your men stopped here," Voyaging Moon said. "That's plain enough."

"Then what?" Mafoo demanded. "Vanished into thin air?"

The girl shrugged. "I see what I see."

"Are there other chambers?" Prince Jen took a torch and paced the length and breadth of the cave. The few recesses and passages were all too shallow and led nowhere.

"I know exactly what happened," Mafoo declared.

"Very simple and logical. They came in. They stopped at the wall. Obviously, they couldn't have gone through it. So, they turned around and left."

"If they did," Voyaging Moon said to Prince Jen, "you'll no doubt ask me to pick up their trail again. All right, as you insist. It's too dark to see anything now. Best stay where we are. In the morning, I'll do what I can."

At her instruction, Mafoo built a fire to keep off the chill of the cavern. From her saddlebag, Voyaging Moon shared some of the food she had extracted from Cha-wei's larder. Prince Jen ate with excellent appetite, feeling in better spirits now than when first setting out. Though he reproached himself for his misjudgment in letting the saddle out of his hands—for all that it had seemed right and sensible at the time—he was confident of finding Li Kwang and seeing the matter finally settled.

Despite his complaining at the hard ground and sharp stones, Mafoo curled up and immediately began snoring. Voyaging Moon stretched out, her jacket rolled up under her head. Prince Jen, who had never reposed on anything harsher than silk, propped his back against the stone wall and found it not unbearable. For a while, he happily observed the sleeping flute girl, and, at last, his eyes closed.

Voices roused him. Voyaging Moon had already leaped to her feet. Prince Jen scrambled up. The torches had burned low; gray morning light filtered through crevices in the ceiling. A tall figure stood in the mouth of the cave. Tied around his head was a bloodstained yellow scarf.

• • • • •

Though Prince Jen is unaware of it, we already know what has happened to Li Kwang. But now is a new disaster about to over-take our three travelers? For the answer, read the following chapter.

7

"BRING LIGHTS HERE." The man, big, rawboned, was dressed in a rag of a shirt and a pair of tattered trousers. A sword hung at his side. Two quick paces and he was inside the cavern. Prince Jen flung a protecting arm around Voyaging Moon. Mafoo, rubbing sleep from his eyes, hurried to join them.

The tall man set his fists on his hips. His face was chalked a deathly white and streaked with crimson; across his brow, a smear of bright yellow. Some half-dozen companions, as roughly garbed and fiercely daubed as their leader, drifted in behind him.

"What have we found?" The man's eyes glittered as one of his comrades held up a lantern. "A farm girl: peasant stock, from the look of her. But these two are a different breed. Town rats, I'd say. That one with a belt too short for his belly has spent some time in dumpling houses. The other's no pauper, not in those fancy clothes. A young idler from a rich family. Father's pride, mother's joy."

"I know of you." Prince Jen looked squarely at him. "Natha Yellow Scarf. The law will deal with you, not I. You are not our concern. Either leave us or let us leave."

"What, you order me?" Natha's eyes blazed. He thrust his face close to Prince Jen's. "Oh, my lad, you say you know of me, but you know me not at all. You have a glib tongue. Mind how it wags. You may lose it."

"What he means to say," Mafoo hastily put in, "is that we're only passing through. Harmless travelers, as you see."

"We, too, are only passing through. The horses outside made me wonder who might be inside. Idle curiosity. We won't inconvenience you more than we need."

"Yes, well, in that case," Mafoo said, "we'll go quietly on our way and about our business. There's nothing you could want—"

"But there is. Indeed, there is. What do I want? Let me think." Natha paced back and forth, chin in hand. He stopped in front of Prince Jen. "Yes. What I need, first, is three good reasons why I shouldn't cut all your throats.

"It should be easy," Natha went on, before Prince Jen could reply. "A moment's thought and you'll have dozens. I ask only three. Nothing comes quickly to mind? Let me start you off."

Natha raised a finger. "One. You'll tell me I'm a kindhearted, easygoing sort of fellow. That's good. I'll accept that.

"Two." He raised another finger. "Why not say, 'It would be a shame to spoil a sunny morning'? All right, I'm in good spirits. We had a little scuffle with some yokels from Kwan-tzu. To celebrate our victory? That's another good reason.

"Two, so far. Now we must seek a third. What can it be?" Natha frowned and shook his head. "Harder than I thought. Yet you must find it.

"Yes, here it is!" He turned to Voyaging Moon. "Third. The farm girl's going to bargain for your lives."

"Stand away from her," Prince Jen burst out. Voyaging Moon made a quick gesture for him to be silent.

"Another order?" Natha snapped. "Why, lad, she may offer me the best reason of all. I've seen prettier, but she may turn out to have a charm all her own."

Voyaging Moon's chin went up. Natha reached out and held her face in a tight grip. "As I take a better look at her, I think we may come to an agreement."

"Let her be." Prince Jen tore Natha's hand away. "Do you want another reason? I'll give you one."

Natha's eyes widened for a moment, then he grinned like a sword pulled from a sheath. In one sudden movement, he struck Prince Jen full in the face.

The blow sent Prince Jen reeling against the cavern wall. Natha's henchmen sprang to surround Voyaging Moon and Mafoo. Stunned, bewildered, Prince Jen put his fingertips to his mouth and stared at the blood staining them. It was not the pain of the blow that shocked him, but that it had been struck at all. He could scarcely comprehend something so monstrous, unthinkable. He drew himself up to his full height.

"How dare you?" He spoke barely above a whisper, but the tone made Natha stop short. "How dare you defile my royal person?"

Prince Jen's voice rose. It rang through the cavern. "Kowtow! To the ground. All. Obey. I am the son of His Divine Majesty. I am Jen Shao-yeh. The Young Lord Prince."

Natha started a moment. Mafoo rolled up his eyes and held his head in dismay. Voyaging Moon broke the sudden silence.

"Don't play the clown," she cried out to Prince Jen. "At a time like this? Silly fool, you'll have us all killed. No more jokes. Be serious for once."

Natha glanced from Prince Jen to Voyaging Moon and back again. He clapped his hands and burst into laughter.

"Why, you truly are a fool! Think yourself clever? Is that your third reason? Oh, no, no, lad. Son of King T'ai? That would be the best reason—to slit your gullet here and now." Natha spat scornfully. "King? As much king as a bundle of straw. The officials are his masters. And ours. And strip us to the bone. Ask the peasant girl."

"And you?" Voyaging Moon said. "You're treating us as badly as any official. We've done you no harm, but you talk of cutting our throats."

"Not yours," Natha said, after a moment, as Voyaging Moon looked steadily at him. She had spoken lightly, but her voice had an edge to it. He turned away, unable to meet her gaze. "To the devil with you." He grimaced. "I had half a mind to take you with me. You'll go free. I think you'd be more trouble than you're worth.

"Even so," Natha went on, "I want my third reason from that pair. Since they can't seem to find one, I'll have to find it for them. Let's consider gold and silver."

"None," said one of his companions. "We've already searched the fat one. Not a purse, not a coin."

"I'll have something for my trouble," Natha cried angrily. His eyes lit on the bundle of gifts by the wall. "What's that?"

"Of no value to you." Prince Jen went to stand in front of the gifts.

"I'll see that for myself." Natha strode after him. He pushed Prince Jen aside and tore away the wrappings.

"What rubbish is this? A paint box? A kite? Are those your playthings?"

That instant, before Natha caught sight of it, Prince Jen snatched up the sword and tore it from the scabbard. Natha halted abruptly. "Ah. Now that's a little more interesting. Hand it over."

Prince Jen's blood had been aboil from the moment Natha had dared to strike him. The sight of the grinning, garishly daubed face, the hand outstretched and fingers twitching, swept away every shred of caution. He had already parted with one gift. He would not part with another.

"No need to shed blood," Natha said soothingly, "neither yours nor mine. You've shown a bold face, you've made the noble gesture. Enough. I need a sword more than you do. Throw it down and there's an end. I won't kill you or the dumpling eater unless I have to. My word on it."

Prince Jen raised the sword point. Seeing their chief threatened, a couple of Natha's companions started forward. Natha waved them away. "We have a fighting cricket here. I can deal with him."

Natha's hand went to his own sword hilt. Prince Jen crouched, ready for the attack. Natha drew out only the jagged stump of a blade.

"I broke this against those Kwan-tzu yokels." Natha tossed aside the shattered weapon. "I must have another. You can't expect me to go unarmed"—Natha spread his empty hands—"not in my trade. We can settle the matter reasonably between us."

Prince Jen had been well instructed in swordplay, but Natha suddenly leaped faster than his eyes could follow. He swung the blade wildly, borne back against the cavern wall. In the instant, Natha seized him by the hair with one hand and by the throat with the other.

"Here's the nub of it," Natha said through clenched teeth. "You try a stab at me. If you can. The question: Will you do it before I snap your neck? Think it over. Quickly. You manage to put that blade in my belly? Do you suppose my people would let you or your friends out of here alive?"

Prince Jen gave a stifled cry as Natha tightened his grip. His stomach heaved, a sickening tide welled into his throat; he was drowning in it. His world had become suddenly very small: only a black whirlpool and his death at the bottom of it. He could not tell whether he was screaming or weeping.

He made a last effort to break free. His head swam, his eyes dimmed. He opened his hand. The sword fell to the ground.

Natha grunted in satisfaction. He threw Prince Jen aside and picked up sword and scabbard. He hefted the weapon, swung it around, then nodded.

"It will serve." Natha motioned toward Mafoo and the half-conscious Prince Jen. "We can use their boots. Take them. The fancy robes, too."

Prince Jen was hardly aware of his robe being stripped away or the boots wrenched from his feet. He crouched against the wall, his head bowed. Natha stared down coldly at him.

"I'd have killed you, had I wished. Like that." Natha snapped his fingers. "You knew it. Death. You smelled it, didn't you? And didn't like the stink of it. Cheer up. None of us does. Be glad I kept my word."

He made an exaggerated bow to Voyaging Moon. "Not for his sake. A small courtesy to you. I hope our paths cross again in pleasanter ways. Meantime, send the boy home to his doting parents."

Natha turned on his heels. His comrades followed him out of the cavern. Voyaging Moon knelt beside Prince Jen and put a hand on his arm.

"Forget the sword. It's gone, and that's that," she said. "You're lucky he didn't break your neck for sheer amusement. You did the only sensible, reasonable thing."

"No." Prince Jen's face burned. "Master Hu would have been ashamed of me. Reason! Sense! It was fear. Only fear."

"Still a good reason," Voyaging Moon said, "and a very common emotion. Your subjects know it well."

"I am not one of my subjects."

"Oh, that's right. I forgot." Voyaging Moon smiled. "Then, count yourself even luckier."

* * * * *

We must now, for the time being, leave Jen unhappy and ashamed so that we can follow Natha Yellow Scarf and the sword he gained. That story is told in the next chapter.

8

· *The Tale of the Thirsty Sword* ·

THE BANDIT NATHA YELLOW SCARF had once been a peasant with a small farm of his own. Bad times fell upon him and he borrowed money from a more prosperous neighbor. This man, however, secretly coveted the land and wanted to add it to his holdings; and so, when the time came to repay, he falsified accounts to make the debt appear triple the sum. Natha pleaded his case in the law court, but the magistrate had been bribed to judge against him. Stripped of house, land, and livestock and left with little more than the shirt on his back, Natha turned to banditry. Others who had suffered like injustices came soon to join him.

From then on, great landowners, high officials, and traveling merchants trembled when the Yellow Scarves, as they called themselves, prowled the countryside. Ruthless though they were, they often shared their plunder with the needy. As a result, the Yellow Scarves were coming to be admired by the poor while feared by the rich.

Now, having taken robes, sword, and horses from the travelers in the cave, the Yellow Scarves galloped off in haste; for the men of Kwan-tzu, regrouping after the earlier skirmish, were still on their heels. Natha intended leading his men into hiding, but a scheme took shape in his mind. He ordered a halt. Leaving his companions to divide the loot, he went off to ponder his idea.

Natha sat down on a boulder. Chewing over questions about his plan, he drew the sword and toyed with it. The hilt fit his hand as if made for it. The keen edge shimmered.

"Fine prize. Better than I thought," he said. He stood and made a few passes in the air. His eye lit on a young pine tree. Thinking to test the blade against it, he swung the sword lightly and easily. It cut through the trunk so swiftly and cleanly that the tree remained standing. Natha stared, hardly believing what he had done.

Their nest disturbed, hornets swarmed out. Natha

waved the sword to fend them off. In a twinkling, the blade sliced them to bits. One angry insect flew at him. The blade seemed to leap instantly and cut it in two.

"This sword grows interesting," Natha said. He laughed and brandished the weapon. "I think we'll get on well together."

He rejoined his companions to find them grumbling and scowling. One, a narrow-faced, hardmouthed fellow called Feng, had decked himself out in Prince Jen's robe.

"We've been well tricked," Feng called out, handing Natha a document that had been tucked away in the garment. "That young fop told the truth."

Natha squinted at the official calligraphy and vermilion seal. He understood it was a royal warrant, its bearer indeed the Young Lord Prince. Some of the Yellow Scarves clamored to go back and lay hands on him, kill him outright, or hold him for ransom.

"Be silent, all of you," burst out Natha, swallowing his anger at being duped. "Go back after him? He's long gone by now. Kill him? No, let him slink home with his tail between his legs. He can tell King T'ai that here, in these mountains, I'm a ruler better than he can ever be. Ransom? What I took is worth as much as any ransom."

Natha tore the warrant to bits and threw the shreds to the ground. He strode some dozen paces away and ordered Feng to shoot an arrow at him.

"Let it fly as near to me as you can. Mind your

aim," Natha said. "Nick me and you'll get a nick from this blade."

Feng, puzzled, did as Natha bade him. He drew his bow and sent a shaft hissing toward his chief. In a trice, Natha swung up the sword and with a quick stroke cut the arrow in two as it sped by him. He did likewise with two more shafts aimed still closer. Now confident, he commanded Feng to loose a third arrow straight at his breast. This, as well, Natha cut to bits with a single stroke before the arrow came near its mark.

The Yellow Scarves gaped in wonder. The astonished Feng, shaking his head, stepped up to Natha.

"What's the trick? How's it done?" Feng reached out. "Give it here. Let me try."

Natha struck Feng's hand away. "Paws off! All of you. This is mine, no other's."

He then called his followers around him and told them his plan, for the sword had given him a resource better than he could have devised. Natha had first intended to make a hasty raid on Kwan-tzu before the village men returned. Now a bolder thought had come to him. The sword seemed to have filled him with such strength and determination that he knew he could not fail.

So, instead of eluding the villagers, Natha and his companions turned and sought them out, soon coming upon them in a clearing where they had stopped to rest. The villagers sprang up and would have beset the Yellow Scarves; but Natha strode to face them, holding aloft the sword and demanding for them to hear him.

His tone and bearing stopped them in their tracks. His voice rang as he addressed them, calling them brothers, reminding them they had never suffered at his hands and many had benefited.

"Now you want to capture and kill us," Natha cried. "Only tell me one thing: What will you gain? Will your wives and children be better fed? Will the merchants and moneylenders be generous to you? Will Cha-wei listen closer to your grievances? Will he give you even grudging thanks?"

"And you?" one of the villagers called out. "What will you give us?"

Natha would have been a commanding figure in any circumstances, but now, sword flashing and his words stirring the villagers' hearts, he seemed to stand even taller. His eyes blazed, his voice thundered:

"What will I give you? Why, brothers, no less than what you deserve. I'll give you Kwan-tzu!"

The villagers roared agreement, shouted allegiance to Natha when they heard what else he promised. And so, joining forces, the Yellow Scarves and their would-be captors galloped back to the village.

There, following Natha's orders, before Cha-wei or any local dignitary understood what was afoot, the villagers broke into the granaries and the storehouses of food and clothing, smashing and burning the shops of any who stood against them. The richest merchants and moneylenders were dragged from their houses, cash boxes pried open, and all their valuables heaped in the public square. Under Natha's instructions, the Yellow Scarves shared out the plunder among the rejoicing villagers, laughing and dancing as if at a festival.

The yamen officials and servants, wailing, weeping, eyes rolling in terror, were also herded into the square. Natha strode back and forth, spitting curses at them for their greed and dishonesty, arrogance and laziness. He declared himself chief of Kwan-tzu and demanded their sworn obedience. If any hesitated for so much as a moment, he turned them over to the rough justice of the crowd.

Those who vowed to serve faithfully and dutifully were set free. Two men remained: Official of the Third Rank Cha-wei, blubbering and kowtowing; and a spice merchant begging for his life, moaning louder than Cha-wei.

"Look at me!" Natha shouted. "Do you know who I am?"

The two stared up at him. Their pleading words shriveled in their throats. They could only nod. For, indeed, Cha-wei was the magistrate who had connived against Natha. The other was the man who had cheated Natha of his landholdings and, profiting from them, had set himself up and made a fortune as a spice merchant.

Natha smiled. "I will be merciful."

With one blow of the sword, he struck off their heads.

That night, Natha lodged in Cha-wei's yamen, in

Cha-wei's apartments, and slept in Cha-wei's bed. Toward dawn, he was roused by a faint voice crying:

"Give me to drink."

Thinking it was one of the servants, wakeful and restless, Natha paid no heed, rolled over, and slept again.

Next day, with the Yellow Scarves in attendance upon him, Natha summoned all villagers with grievances to declare them and have them redressed. Some who came complained of having been cheated in business transactions, others of being given short weight from dishonest scales, still others whose petitions had been ignored. Natha heard each one and decided each case fairly.

The last man appeared uneasy and reluctant to speak. Finally, at Natha's urging, he drew himself up and stated:

"Honorable Sir, when the goods were shared out, someone laid hands on much more than his proper portion. Also, he forced others to give him many strings of cash."

Several witnesses came forward to bear out this testimony. Natha replied angrily that such conduct called for severe punishment and demanded the name of the criminal.

"Honorable Sir," the villager stammered, "it was a Yellow Scarf—one of your own men." He pointed toward Feng, standing by Natha in the Chamber of Audience.

Natha turned to Feng. "True?"

Feng shrugged. "What do villagers need with all that cash? Without us, they'd have had nothing. We deserve the greater share."

"You acted no better than Cha-wei or any greedy official," Natha retorted. "This is my judgment."

He leaped to his feet, drew the sword, and, before Feng could speak further, cut him down on the spot. The Yellow Scarves, outraged, started toward Natha; but he threatened them with the sword and declared he had done only simple justice. In the end, fearing his wrath, they agreed it was so. Natha ordered Feng's head hung at the yamen gate as a warning to all who dealt unjustly with their fellows.

Again that night, Natha was awakened by the same voice crying:

"Give me to drink."

Natha sprang up. The voice seemed to be in the chamber. He lit a lamp and, suspecting some treachery, peered into every corner and cabinet. The voice called out once more. Natha stopped short. He turned his gaze upon the sword, for the words had come from it.

Frightened at first, Natha raised a hand to ward off any ghost or demon. But the sword whispered and murmured so cajolingly and with such plaintive insistence that his fear quickly vanished. He sat down on the bed, the sword across his knees.

"What are you?" he asked, in wonder. "Why do you speak? What do you want of me?"

The sword only replied, "Give me to drink."

Natha questioned it no further. He felt sure now that some marvelous thing had come into his hands.

"And why?" he asked himself. "Clearly, because I alone deserve to wield it."

Natha said nothing of this to any of his companions. In the days following, however, he kept himself a little apart from them, the sword ever at hand. The Yellow Scarves wondered about this behavior but dared not question him, for the forbidding look on Natha's face warned them off. Nevertheless, Natha governed more justly than Cha-wei or any official had.

At this time, word reached Natha that the prefect of the district, learning of the happenings in Kwan-tzu, had sent a strong force of warriors to recapture the village. That night, Natha pondered what best to do, and if he should withdraw and lead his Yellow Scarves to a safe hiding place in the uplands. Deep in thought, turning questions over in his mind, Natha was roused by the insistent voice:

"Give me to drink."

"Yes!" cried Natha. "So I will!"

Next day, Natha ordered his Yellow Scarves and all the men he could muster out of Kwan-tzu. Instead of retreating at the approach of the warriors, Natha struck first. He himself galloped foremost into the fray, and laid about him ferociously with the sword, cutting down so many of his opponents that the rest, in terror and despair, flung away their weapons and surrendered to him. As he had done before with the villagers, Natha offered to spare their lives if they would swear allegiance to him. This they gladly did, and Natha led them all triumphantly to Kwan-tzu.

But now, with such a number of new followers, Natha was hard-pressed for provisions to feed them. Though he required the villagers to give up much of their own small stores of food, it was not enough. Villagers and warriors alike grew hungry and restless, and some began muttering doubts about Natha's wisdom.

"Give me to drink," the sword whispered.

And Natha called a party of warriors to him and led them into the countryside, demanding victuals from the peasant farmers and tribute from the smallest hamlets. Where Natha once shared his takings, he demanded these folk to empty most of their larders. Some did so, but many refused. From them, Natha carried off all they had, burned their farmhouses as an example to the others; and, if any raised hand or voice against him, he slew them.

The poorest found their only hope in joining his growing forces, but this in turn obliged him to plunder still farther afield.

Always, the sword murmured, "Give me to drink."

The provincial governor, alarmed to learn that Natha Yellow Scarf had come to hold sway over much of the region, determined to settle the matter once and for all. He ordered every warrior at his disposal to advance on Kwan-tzu, crush this challenge to his authority, and take Natha dead or alive.

Reports of the heavily armed force soon came to Natha. For the first time, his resolution faltered. He knew his followers were greatly outnumbered; he doubted that even he could convince such an army to join him. Prudence dictated retreat. About to give that order, he heard the voice of the sword:

"Give me to drink."

And so, once more, he led out his men. They fell upon the governor's warriors as Natha plunged into the thick of the fight like a maddened tiger. Those who saw him that day believed he had grown gigantic in stature and his horse had become a dragon. Foam flecked Natha's lips, his frenzied roars drowned out the din of battle as the sword flashed in lightning bolts, hewing and slashing, cutting down all before him, pursuing and killing even those who fled in terror.

Before the day was out, the provincial troops broke in panic and scattered, leaving their dead and wounded behind them.

Natha, spattered with the blood of his enemies, galloped to the crest of a little hill, where he threw back his head and laughed in jubilation at the sight of the shattered army.

"Who can stand against me?" he cried. He started to signal a return to Kwan-tzu, then halted and spat scornfully.

"One wretched village?" he said. "A handful of

miserable peasants? Is that to be my realm? Pitiful! Shall I choose to be so small? Why not choose to be great?"

The sword whispered:

"Give me to drink."

．　．　．　．　．

What becomes of Natha Yellow Scarf lies hidden in the future. For now, we go back to Prince Jen and his friends where we left them in the cavern. Robbed and terrorized by bandits, they are worse off than ever. What can they possibly do? That is told in the next chapter.

9

"MY WARRANT'S GONE!" Only now did Prince Jen realize that more than the sword had been taken. Stripping him of his robe, the bandits had also made off with his royal identification and authority.

"Never mind that. You can't ride a scrap of paper." Mafoo shook his fist at the Yellow Scarves, who had already galloped out of sight. "Sons of turtles! They stole our horses!"

In the course of what had at first promised to be a pleasantly interesting journey, Prince Jen, so far, had

been half drowned, mired in mud, and imposed on by a
disgusting old crackpot; and now robbed, terrorized,
and forced to gulp down shame enough to last a lifetime. Even a gentle-natured prince has a limited store
of tolerance, and Prince Jen, blood in his eye and ferocious thoughts in his head, was set on personally throttling Natha and all his band as well. He jumped to his
feet and started for the mouth of the cavern.

"Jen!"

He was partway down the path when this call from
Voyaging Moon brought him up short. Somehow it
pleased him that she had overlooked the royal title.

"Young Lord Prince—" Voyaging Moon corrected
herself.

"No. Only call me 'prince' when I get back my
warrant. And the saddle. And the sword."

"If you like," Voyaging Moon said. "It does save
time. Now that you've calmed down a little and started
thinking sensibly, you've already figured it out. Find Li
Kwang and you'll have that saddle you say is so important. Then, with him and his troops, you'll have a better chance of following the Yellow Scarves and getting
the sword from Natha."

"I want more than that from him," Jen muttered
between his teeth. He went back and bundled up the
remaining gifts. He hurried from the cavern and, with
Voyaging Moon, set about finding the warriors' tracks.

"Ai-yah! Ai-yah!" Trying to keep up with his master and the flute girl, Mafoo hopped as if he were cross-

ing a bed of hot coals. "My feet aren't used to this torture. I wish those devils had taken my trousers instead of my boots."

Jen, for his part, paid no heed to the stones that bruised and bloodied his own unshod feet. While Voyaging Moon searched in one direction, he pressed farther ahead in another, with no success. Though it was now full daylight, the girl's quick eyes caught no trace of the vanished escort.

"Mafoo thought they doubled back," Jen called. "Could they have gone all the way down again?"

No longer content to let the flute girl take the lead, Jen ordered Voyaging Moon to quarter one side of the path and Mafoo the other, then set off practically racing downhill.

"He's acting more like a prince without that warrant than he did when he had it," Mafoo groaned, trying to rub his feet and walk at the same time. "Life was less strenuous before he decided to take charge of things."

Late in the day, when the travelers came back to the roadside, they found no sign that Li Kwang and his men had ever returned. Mafoo hunkered down in the bushes and comforted his toes. Jen and Voyaging Moon gave one last, fruitless search. The girl's spirits had not flagged until now, when she wearily admitted she could do no more.

"Not a footprint. Not a hoofprint," she said. "We've lost them for good."

"Then what?" Jen's vision of courageously regaining the sword was rapidly fading. Li Kwang might as well have disappeared from the face of the earth. What grew clear, instead, was that he had little chance of recovering the saddle or the sword. "We can't stand here in the middle of the road."

"Yes, we can," Mafoo said, "until my blisters heal."

"Is there a village nearby? A farmhouse?" Jen asked Voyaging Moon. "Anyplace at all we can shelter?"

"I'm out of my district," the girl said. "I don't know this part of the province."

"We'll keep on until we find something."

"And when you do?" Voyaging Moon said. "You'll make a grand procession with your band of retainers, all two of them. And the royal prince himself—I'm sure you'll forgive me for pointing this out—looking like the king of scarecrows. You can explain everything, of course; and why you haven't a scrap of evidence to prove it. Also, it's going to be dark. Do you mean to go hacking through the countryside all night?"

"I admire your line of reasoning," Mafoo said, beaming. "The most practical thing at the moment is the simplest: sit down."

Jen bristled. The girl nettled him, as did Mafoo for agreeing with her. Nevertheless, he had no ready answer. He reluctantly followed Mafoo a little way off the road. Like a dog making its bed, Mafoo flattened a space in the undergrowth and curled up in one corner. Resigned to spending the night, Jen dropped the bundle of gifts, much lighter than before, and sat cross-legged beside it.

"Mafoo warned me," Jen said, as Voyaging Moon settled next to him. "He didn't want to go to T'ien-kuo, and he didn't want me to do it either. I should have listened to him. What do I know of learning to govern? Or taking charge of Yuan-ming's gifts? I've already lost two of them. Someone else should have gone in my place. Who, I don't know. I think anyone would have done better."

"You can still make your way back to Ch'ang-an," Voyaging Moon said.

"Yes. In disgrace," Jen said. "Shall I tell my father I failed before I barely started? He trusted me to do what he wasn't able to do. Shall I tell him how frightened I was? A sorry sort of courage for a prince."

"A prince isn't required to be a fool," Voyaging Moon said. "Anyone would have done the same. Show courage by letting some hulking ruffian snap your neck? Brave? I'd call it plainly stupid. Anyhow, what you do next has to be up to you."

"Suppose I went to Kwan-tzu?" Jen said, after a time. "Cha-wei knows he's obliged to give me provisions, horses, everything we need. Don't worry about him," he added. "I'll tell him you're under my protection. Like it or not, he won't dare do anything."

"He's tricky," Voyaging Moon said. "I don't like the idea of being anywhere near him."

"What else then? We need food, water, clothing.

Now we have nothing." Jen glanced at the small bundle. "Only these, and they're no help to us. Valuable gifts? Natha called them playthings."

He undid the wrappings. "I wonder why Master Wu chose them. Worthy offerings for a great king?" He picked up the flute and smiled at Voyaging Moon. "This makes me think of that night in Cha-wei's yamen. You played beautifully. I'd never heard anything like it. Please play again."

Voyaging Moon put the flute to her lips. Instantly, the notes rose and hovered gently in the air. She stopped, surprised. "It hardly needs a breath. I don't know about the other gifts, but this one—Master Wu chose it well."

The girl began once more. At the first floating strands of melody, Jen felt his heart lighten. Within moments, his humiliation at the hands of Natha, his dismay at Li Kwang's disappearance, his failure to guard the offerings all turned weightless, borne away by the song of the flute.

As for Voyaging Moon, he could scarcely believe this was the same girl, barefoot, in coarse garments, with her high-cheeked peasant features. Her face shone with a golden light in the rays of the setting sun. Watching her, he felt she might vanish at any moment, carried off on the stream of music. He hardly dared to breathe. He sat motionless, hands folded, eyes lowered.

Mafoo stirred and raised himself on an elbow. "Marvelous!" He sighed. "It made me dream of dumplings."

Voyaging Moon laughed. The spell was broken. She put down the flute. Jen urged her to keep on. She shook her head sadly.

"This is not mine to play."

"It must be given to Yuan-ming, if ever I reach him," Jen said, his voice heavy with regret. "It is not mine, either. Until I have to part with it, I leave it in your hands, to play as you will. This gift, at least, is worthy—"

Voyaging Moon put a finger to her lips. "Quiet. Careful," she whispered. "Don't move suddenly. Something's behind us in the bushes."

＊ ＊ ＊ ＊ ＊

What now? Does yet another danger threaten our hero and his friends? To find out, go quickly to the next chapter.

10

JEN SPRANG TO HIS FEET. For an instant, he feared one of the Yellow Scarves had come back. He threw himself at the black-garbed figure. Voyaging Moon and Mafoo instantly followed, wrestling the intruder to the ground.

Finding himself so briskly set upon, the man produced a number of bloodcurdling yells. Eyes rolling in terror, his long, ropy hair swinging wildly, he turned and twisted in every effort to shake free. By then, Mafoo had clutched him by the ears, and Voyaging Moon had gripped the collar of his long-tailed shirt;

their opponent, all the while, bawled indignantly: "Be calm! Be calm! I only want to rob you!"

"That," burst out Jen, "is all I need to hear!"

"Turtle!" Mafoo shouted. "Son of a turtle! You'll get something you didn't bargain for."

"Leave us alone," Voyaging Moon ordered. "We've been robbed already."

"Oh? You have?" The man stopped struggling. "Never mind, then. My humblest apologies."

"Let him up," Jen told Mafoo, who had taken a seat on the would-be robber's chest. "Whatever he is, he's no Yellow Scarf."

"Certainly not," the man replied, in a wounded tone. "Honorable sirs and lady, you do me a grave injustice if you think I have any part of them. That gang of lawless ruffians? No, no, I go about my business according to the highest standards of conduct, the Precepts of Honorable Robbery. Ask anybody. You'll hear nothing but favorable reports of Moxa. Or, if you prefer, the Mad Robber."

"I never knew of a robber apologizing, that's true enough," Voyaging Moon remarked.

"I made an unfortunate error. But how could I have guessed?" Moxa sat up and rubbed his ears. In the tattered black shirt that hung below his knees, the ropes of hair drooping below his shoulders, the self-styled Mad Robber appeared more poverty-stricken than mad. He was thin as a rail, with lanky legs, bony arms, and sharp elbows. His attempt at growing a mustache had clearly failed; he had sprouted only a few reluctant hairs, giving his face the look of a starved cat with a very large spider sitting on its head.

"I'm happy to advise you," Moxa continued, "you qualify under the Precepts, which I consider inviolable. In all my career, I have never broken one of them."

"What are you telling us?" Jen asked. "Robbers have precepts?"

"Hardly any. That is, none at all. Not in these times. They have no respect for decency and tradition. Except my humble self. Centuries ago, the Great Robber Kwen-louen laid down the Precepts, which I follow as a matter of moral principle. The one that applies to you is: Never rob someone who has already been robbed; as they are already distraught, it would be heartless to make them feel worse.

"As for the others," Moxa added, "never rob the poor, for that would only add to their misery. Never rob someone you know, for that would be treacherous. Never rob the happy, celebrating some good fortune, say a birthday or a wedding, for that would spoil their moment of joy. By the same token, never rob the unhappy, which would make them lose hope altogether."

"That leaves only rich strangers?" said Jen, who had been listening with curiosity to Moxa's explanation.

"Exactly. Unless, of course, the other Precepts apply. A rich stranger may be as unhappy as a poor acquaintance; or have just been robbed; and so on."

"You don't look as though your Precepts are any help to you," Voyaging Moon observed.

"It's difficult to find suitable candidates," Moxa

agreed. "When you come down to it, most of them are exempt for one reason or another. No matter. I scrupulously obey the Precepts. Otherwise—why, I'd be no more than a common thief.

"But the fact is I didn't mean to rob you. Not at first. No, it was the flute. I was merely passing by when I heard it. Skulking and lurking as befits a robber, you understand. And what strikes my Ear of Continual Attentiveness?" Moxa tugged at one of his remarkably large appendages. "Music! Marvelous! Irresistible! It seized hold of me, pulled me along. I had to hear more.

"You were the one playing," Moxa said, with an adoring glance at Voyaging Moon. He jumped to his feet, eyes alight. "Amazing sensation! It made me think of home and loved ones. Not that I ever had any, but I thought of them, even so. And all manner of joyful things that never happened to me but seemed as if they should have. When you stopped playing," he added, "I thought: Ah, well, I'll practice my profession since I'm here. Nothing malicious, we all have to live as best we can. You didn't have to kick me. Or sit on me. Not necessary."

Moxa broke off suddenly. "Have you eaten?"

"We can't feed you," Jen said. "You'll have to find someone better provisioned than we are."

"I didn't mean that," Moxa said. "I meant that if you haven't eaten within recent memory—as my Eye of Discerning Perception tells me may be the case—I'll be happy to share what I have."

With that, the robber pulled out a sack he had

dropped in the bushes. He rummaged in it, dredging up knotted cords, iron hooks, strips of wood, and a jumble of objects that Jen could not begin to identify. At last, he retrieved a handful of dry morsels and eagerly passed them around. With the efficiency of long practice, he scooped up twigs and dry branches and, within moments, lit a cheerful fire; all the while, like a host at a feast, he urged his guests to enjoy their food.

Biting into the leathery substance, Jen could not decide whether it was fish that had been too long in company with a chicken or the other way round. His hunger, nevertheless, had grown sharp, and he gnawed away gratefully.

"This won't keep us long from starvation," he murmured to Mafoo, who had downed his portion in one gulp. "I don't see any better course. We'll have to go to Kwan-tzu."

"What? What? Where?" Moxa exclaimed, cupping his Ear of Continual Attentiveness. "Kwan-tzu, did you say? Not the best of places. Not now."

"If you don't mind," Mafoo said, with a hard glance at the robber, "this is a private discussion. It doesn't concern you."

"Of course not, of course not, if you say so," Moxa replied. "But I can tell you this: While I was skulking and lurking, I came across those Yellow Scarves. And a band of villagers. I hid and listened to them. Trouble in the wind. The Nose of Thoughtful Inhalations sniffed it instantly. The Voice of Solemn Warning"—Moxa lowered his tone—"says: Keep away."

"The Yellow Scarves are the ones who robbed us," Jen said. "They took something from me. I want it back."

"Whatever it is, you won't get it," Moxa replied. "My Ear of Continual Attentiveness told me they're going to capture the town and kill the officials, the merchants—anybody who isn't with them. Go there and you won't come out again.

"On the other hand," Moxa continued, his eyes brightening and his cat's whiskers twitching, "the Voice of Daring Enterprise says: Why not?" Moxa waved his arms. "We dash in, take them by surprise, fight our way out, hacking right and left—do you have anything to hack with?—then, triumphant celebration! Do it! Risk all! Magnificent!"

"Lunatic!" snapped Mafoo. "I have a voice, too. I call it the Voice of Plain Common Sense. It tells me: Don't look for trouble, we've had enough already."

"Mafoo's right," Jen said, after some moments of thought. Moxa, deflated, went back to munching his food. "Very well," Jen added, "we won't go there. But then what?"

"Young Lord," Mafoo began, "it seems to me—"

"What was that?" Moxa stopped in midmunch. "What did you say? You called him—"

"Keep your Ear of Continual Attentiveness to yourself," Mafoo retorted, "and your Nose of Whatever out of other people's business."

"Young Lord? Young Lord?" Moxa's agitation grew. "There were rumors of—Prince Jen! You're the son of King T'ai? The prince himself? In this condition?"

Jen nodded.

"What have I done?" Moxa clapped his hands to his head. "Assaulted a Royal Person! Monstrous! Horrible! A capital crime! Oh, misery! Oh, death! Sliced to bits, cut to pieces!

"Worse, I've broken a Precept!" Moxa wailed. "There's yet another: Never assault the Divine King or his offspring, it shows lack of respect. I'd put it out of my mind, almost forgotten. No likelihood of its happening. But it has happened. Unpardonable! Unforgivable!"

"Don't upset yourself," Jen said, trying to calm the despairing robber, whose howls grew louder with each breath. "I was the one who assaulted you. So, you aren't the one who broke a Precept. In any case, it doesn't matter. Because I officially forgive you."

"You do?" Moxa left off his wailing to stare open-mouthed. "You really do?" He flung himself at Jen's feet. "No one's ever forgiven me for anything! My life is yours!"

"Not necessary—" Jen began.

"I insist!" cried Moxa. "Wherever you go, whatever you wish, the Hand of Enthusiastic Obedience, the Heart of Eternal Devotion will serve you."

"Don't think me ungrateful," Jen replied, "but there's no way you can help us. For one thing, I don't even know where we're going. We started out for T'ien-kuo—"

"T'ien-kuo?" cried Moxa. "That marvelous king-dom? I've heard of it since I was a child—at least, I think I did. The tales said it was far to the north. If it exists in the first place. You're going there? Lord Prince, why would you undertake such a journey?"

Despite Mafoo's disapproving frown, Jen explained his mission and told the robber what had befallen them since leaving Ch'ang-an.

"All the more reason for me to serve you," Moxa declared. "I can guide you partway. It's not for the likes of me to set foot in such a place. No robbers al-lowed, I'm sure. But I'll take you as far as I can. The Eye of Perpetual Vigilance will watch over you. Start-ing this moment."

Before Jen could answer one way or the other, Moxa loped to the fringe of the bushes, folded his skinny arms, and stationed himself as motionless as a statue, peering into the rapidly gathering darkness.

"It's not such a bad idea, having him along," Voyaging Moon said. "If we need protection, a rob-ber's as good as anyone."

"He's a maniac," Mafoo retorted. "Eye of Perpetual Vigilance, is it? Yes, well, I'll want to keep my own eye on that fellow."

"I think he's going with us whether we like it or not," Jen said. "Maniac he may be, I'm glad for any help, as things stand now. Let him stay."

Since there seemed to be no alternative, Jen resigned himself to spending the night outdoors. Voyaging Moon, wakeful, sat watching the embers; but Jen, to his surprise, found himself drifting off to sleep as soon as his head touched the ground.

It was daylight when he opened his eyes again. Voyaging Moon, up and about, pointed to the pair of figures.

"Moxa hasn't moved from the spot," she said. "He's watched over us, as he said he would. And Mafoo's been watching over *him*. Between the two, we've been well guarded."

Seeing his master awake, Mafoo came to join him. Moxa, about to do the same, halted and cupped his ear.

"Hark!" he cried. "Does the Ear of Continual Attentiveness hear the sound of horses? What can that mean? I'll find out."

"Wait," Jen called, "what are you going to do?"

"If they're travelers," Moxa said, with a snaggletoothed grin of happy anticipation, "I'll rob them, of course. But—no, no, I won't rob them. You will."

◆　◆　◆　◆　◆

Will our hero, already a victim of bandits, turn bandit himself? Will the Mad Robber lead our friends into still more trouble? The answers are found in the following chapter.

11

*   *Honorable Fat-choy* *
*   *Moxa delves into his sack* *
*   *The Collar of Punishment* *

"YOU'LL DO THE ACTUAL ROBBING," Moxa went on. "As a precaution, you understand. Since it's not your profession, you aren't bound by the Precepts. Whereas if I do it, there's always a chance the candidate may qualify for exemption and I'd have to let him go."

"Moxa," Jen said, "I'm not robbing anybody. There's no way I can do that."

"A dozen ways," Moxa said. "Don't worry. Nothing to it, you'll see. As an amateur, you needn't concern yourself with refinements and niceties. I'll be there, of course. Not in a professional capacity, only to give small pointers when required."

Before Voyaging Moon and Mafoo could offer their own opinions, Moxa seized Jen by the arm and eagerly hurried him into the underbrush. The robber flung himself onto the ground and peered through the tall grass. Moxa's Ear of Continual Attentiveness had not deceived him. Within a few moments, Jen glimpsed a procession of some dozen attendants on foot, a supply cart, and a couple of pack mules. At the head rolled a boxy, two-wheeled carriage, its curtains drawn.

"All we really want is food. Anything else would be a nice little extra," Moxa said. "But, this being your first time out, don't bother about money, trinkets, that sort of thing. People get too upset when it comes to losing their valuables. The main thing is to halt the carriage. I'll do the rest. Any pretext will serve. Tell them your grandmother has colic, tell them—whatever comes to mind. Or do you prefer armed assault?"

"Lunatic!" Mafoo cried. "You'll get us deeper in a mess. Go rob them yourself. Better yet, just go."

"We need food, no question about it," Voyaging Moon told Jen, "but the simplest thing would be to ask."

"You say 'ask'?" Moxa exclaimed. "The Ear of Continual Attentiveness hears 'beg.' What, the Young Lord Prince turns beggar? Please maintain dignity. Propriety. Begging, indeed!"

"Safer than robbing," Voyaging Moon replied.

"If it weren't for the Precepts, I'd do the work myself," said Moxa, whose face had lit up and whose Nose of Thoughtful Inhalations had begun trembling with excitement. "What's to go wrong? Here you have the most elementary type of robbery. The great Kwen-louen named it Bee Approaches Tiger Lily. Simple. Straightforward. Compared with breaking and entering—"

By this time, the procession had drawn close enough for Jen to read the calligraphy on the fluttering red banners proclaiming this to be the entourage of Official of the First Rank Fat-choy. With a cry of relief, Jen sprang to his feet.

"Now, once you're there," Moxa went on, "the first thing to do—"

Jen had already started through the bushes. He motioned for Voyaging Moon and Mafoo to stay back. "Keep Moxa out of sight," he called, hastening toward the road. "This could be a palace official. I'll deal with him myself."

He ran down the slope and broke through the undergrowth, hurrying to overtake the procession. Waving his arms, shouting at them to halt, he headed for Fat-choy's carriage. A pair of attendants blocked his path, angrily warning him away. Jen pressed on, calling out to Fat-choy, demanding assistance in the name of King T'ai.

With the attendants gabbling and clutching at him, Jen shouldered his way to the carriage. As the surprised driver reined up, the curtains shot open and Official of the First Rank Fat-choy himself popped out his head.

"Why stop?" Fat-choy's head, bald as a lemon, took up most of the window. His jowls overflowed his high-necked collar, his eyes bulged out at the sight of Jen, and he began puffing and wheezing with indignation. "What does this mean? Disgusting individual, how dare you approach me?"

"Do you come from Ch'ang-an?" Jen demanded. "The Celestial Palace? You know me, then. I require your help. I am the Young Lord Prince."

Fat-choy pursed his lips. As he looked Jen up and down, his indignation turned to amusement. "What good fortune is mine, to meet such an exalted person-age. No doubt you are in disguise, for reasons best known to your royal self."

"Thank heaven you recognize me." Jen heaved a sigh of relief. "When did you leave Ch'ang-an? How is my father?"

"For one thing," Fat-choy replied, "I am not at-tached to the Celestial Palace. Since you are gracious enough to inquire, allow me to inform you that I have been transferred from Feng-sia to be chief magistrate of Chai-sang.

"For another," Fat-choy continued, "you must admit that it is highly unusual to find the Young Lord suddenly appearing out of nowhere. Forgive me if I restrain my joy until I first beg to inquire how this has come about."

Fat-choy spread a fan and waved it lazily while Jen explained what had brought him to such a state.

"Naturally," Fat-choy said when Jen finished his account, "you can offer some small proof of these most remarkable statements."

"I told you my warrant was stolen," Jen said, with some impatience. "What proof? I have my servant—"

"Enough." Fat-choy gave Jen an oily smile and snapped the fan shut. "As a magistrate, it is my profession and my skill to distinguish between truth and falsehood. I have listened with undivided attention and the highest degree of interest in your testimony and have reached the only proper and correct conclusion. You shall be granted what you require, what you clearly deserve and to which you are fully entitled.

"You asked if I recognized you," Fat-choy went on, beckoning to his attendants. "Although I have not seen you before, I know you very well indeed. That is to say, I know you for a barefaced, insolent liar." Fat-choy turned to one of the servants. "Take this dog and beat him thoroughly."

Before Jen could make a move, one of the retainers seized him by the hair and flung him to his knees while the other belabored him with a bamboo rod. Shouting with pain and outrage, Jen fought to break free. Fat-choy's retainer doubled the blows. Struggling, gasping for breath, Jen ground his teeth in useless fury.

"Lay on, lay on," Fat-choy urged, watching with a critical eye. "Diligence is a virtue. He thought to take advantage of my good nature. He should be grateful his punishment is not worse."

All that kept Jen from howling like an animal was his refusal to give Fat-choy added satisfaction. As the blows continued to rain relentlessly, Jen bit his lips, spat out blood and curses, while Fat-choy smiled and nodded, ordering his retainer to apply the rod more vigorously.

Jen felt himself spinning into unconsciousness when explosions ripped the air. The horses reared in alarm. Fat-choy dropped his fan, his chin collapsed into his neck. As the explosions continued, a gaunt figure bounded into the roadway. Shrieking horribly, shirt flapping, his ropy hair whirling about his head, Moxa leaped and spun like an acrobat, kicking out his legs, flinging himself against the terrified retainers.

Fat-choy regained his wits long enough to consider his immediate well-being. He bellowed for his driver to speed for their lives, popped his head back into the carriage, and snapped the curtain shut. The horses plunged ahead, the retainers took to their heels, and the disarrayed procession went scrambling down the road in a cloud of red dust.

Next thing Jen knew, Voyaging Moon's arms were around him. Dizzy and breathless, his back feeling as if it had been rolled in hot coals, he tried to sit up while Moxa cavorted triumphantly, making impudent gestures at the departing carriage.

"Magnificent!" The gleeful robber turned his attention to Jen. "Never anything so splendid!"

"Are you out of your mind?" retorted Voyaging Moon, who had begun peeling off Jen's shirt to examine his injuries. "Look what they've done."

"Yes, marvelous, isn't it?" Moxa wobbled his head in admiration. "The Young Lord's brilliant inspiration! Who would have thought of getting yourself beaten to distract the candidate? A completely new technique. I must add it to my list. Call it Butterfly Dares Lightning."

"What exploded?" asked Jen as Voyaging Moon dabbed at his back. "It kept Fat-choy from taking off the rest of my skin, whatever it was."

"Firecrackers," Moxa said happily. "I always carry them in my sack. Part of my stock in trade. They do produce a lively effect, don't they?"

Mafoo, clucking anxiously like a bandy-legged hen, had meantime hustled to his master's side. He and Voyaging Moon helped Jen off the road while Moxa retrieved his sack and rummaged out a jar of ointment.

"I keep it on hand for scrapes and bruises," the robber said. "I gather a number in my profession."

"No doubt," Jen said glumly as Voyaging Moon gently rubbed the salve over his shoulders. "I've gathered a number, too, with nothing else to show for it."

"I wouldn't say that," put in Mafoo. "While our flute girl was setting off those firecrackers, and that madman was jumping up and down, I made off with the provisions." Mafoo's lumpy face broke into a proud grin as he motioned toward a horse and a cart full of

victuals. "Fat-choy won't eat much today. But we
will."

Instead of continuing immediately on their way,
Voyaging Moon urged waiting until next day, and Jen
was glad to agree. Despite Moxa's ointment, his back
still throbbed, and he had turned a little feverish. He
ate nothing of the meal Mafoo prepared, but slept fit-
fully, with Voyaging Moon at his side to calm him
when he started up from a troubled dream. At nightfall,
the girl took the flute from the bundle of gifts. As she
played, the voice of the flute seemed to ease his injuries
better than Moxa's ointment. He no longer reproached
himself for having lost two of the valuable objects, and
as his strength came back, he was eager to begin afresh.
He felt confident of reaching the end of his journey,
but his thoughts turned more to Voyaging Moon than
to T'ien-kuo.

Next day, with Moxa striding out ahead, Mafoo
and the cart bringing up the rear, Jen and Voyaging
Moon walked along easily, side by side, hand in hand.
After a time, however, Voyaging Moon began glancing
at the sun and frowning with some perplexity. She
called out to Moxa, who came loping back, cheerfully
grinning.

"Explain something to me," Voyaging Moon said.
"T'ien-kuo's north, isn't it? Why are you taking us
west?"

Moxa blinked at her as if astonished by such a question. "Because the road's better, of course."

"Wait a minute," put in Jen, alarmed. "You're taking us in the wrong direction just because of a good road?"

"Naturally," Moxa said. "I'd be a fool to follow a bad one, wouldn't I? It's the nature of roads to turn, as this one's bound to do. I'm not in the least worried about it."

Mafoo by this time had come up to them. When he heard the robber's explanation, he dropped the horse's halter and seized Moxa by the shirtfront.

"Come straight out with it, you idiot!" cried Mafoo. "You don't have any idea where you're going."

"I do, I do!" Moxa protested. "We'll find our way, you'll see."

The two would have kept on squabbling, but Jen ordered both to silence. Hobbling down the road came an old man barely able to support himself on the staff he carried.

Jen stared, taken aback at the sight; for the man's head, covered with long white hair, matted and befouled, thrust out from a hole in a heavy square of wood wider than his frail shoulders.

"Avoid him!" Moxa turned his eyes away. "Don't go near. He wears the cangue, the Collar of Punishment."

Jen and Voyaging Moon, however, had already started down the road. "What punishment is this?" Jen murmured, appalled. "The cangue? I've never heard of it."

"Not likely you would," Voyaging Moon said. "A prince isn't expected to concern himself with small legal details."

As they drew nearer, Jen cried out in dismay. Despite the old man's blistered, sun-blackened face, Jen thought for an instant that he recognized him.

"Master Wu? No—it can't be. Master Fu?" Jen stopped short and looked again. His eyes had deceived him; it was neither.

For his part, the haggard old man peered sharply at Jen. "Why do you thus address me? I am Master Shu. And you? Are you the one I seek?"

"Who's done this to you? Why?" Jen bent closer. "Never mind that now. We'll get that collar off, to begin with."

"Beware." Master Shu raised a hand in warning. "My cangue is bolted, sealed with a magistrate's seal. It means a death sentence for the one who tampers with it. You know the law."

"I don't know it, but it won't be a law any longer, not if I have any say about it," Jen replied. "Whatever you've done, you'll be free of this collar. By my royal command. I'm Jen Shao-yeh, the Young Lord Prince."

"Are you, indeed? So much the better." Master Shu narrowed his eyes. He studied Jen for a moment, then spat in his face.

• • • • •

What ingratitude is this? By now, our hero should have learned caution in identifying himself to strangers. But who is Master Shu? What crime deserves such horrible punishment? Who is Master Shu seeking? The answers to these and other questions are found in the next chapter.

12

· Reason for Master Shu's discourtesy ·
· The wrong road ·
· Master Shu's advice ·

"THERE," SAID MASTER SHU. "I hope you are sufficiently insulted and infuriated. If not, I shall find some other way to anger you. Have you suggestions?"

Jen, too shocked to reply, had stepped back. Despite his reminding himself that this was a feeble old man, his chin shot up and his eyes flashed. Having recently been beaten with a stick, he was not in a frame of mind to be spat upon, least of all when he intended a kindness.

"Excellent," said Master Shu. "I perceive definite evidence of irritation. By all means, nourish it. When it grows ripe enough, you might care to pick up one of those large rocks over there. Or do you own some weapon? I would prefer it to be sharp-edged and quick."

"Don't let him bait you," Voyaging Moon murmured to Jen, who was still making an effort to keep his temper. "I know what he wants you to do."

"You seem to have grasped my purpose quicker than your companion," Master Shu said. "If he will not oblige me, perhaps you will."

"What purpose?" Jen demanded. "To begin, why insult me? You have no reason."

"Indeed, I do," Master Shu said. "First, if you are the Young Lord Prince, as you claim, you deserve to be insulted for allowing such atrocities as this"—he indicated his wooden collar—"to exist in your kingdom."

"Not my doing," Jen protested. "Palace officials deal with laws. I know nothing of them."

"My point exactly," Master Shu said. "Second, no matter who you are, I hoped you would be furious enough to put me out of my misery. I will beg no one to release me from this cangue; that would set his own life at risk. Therefore, my alternative has been to seek someone who will do me the inestimable favor of dispatching me as rapidly as possible. Now, before your temper cools, please get on with it."

"I have the authority to free you," Jen said. "I'm the Young Lord Prince, whether you believe me or not."

"Oh, I believe you," Master Shu said. "What sane

person would claim to be prince of such a kingdom as ours? Since you appear more or less in possession of your faculties, I conclude you have told the truth."

As Jen wondered whether to take Master Shu's logic as yet another insult, Voyaging Moon beckoned to Moxa, who had been cautiously keeping his distance.

"The Voice of Prudent Obedience tells me not to meddle with the law, no more than I've already done," said Moxa, when Voyaging Moon asked if he had means of breaking the bolts holding the collar shut. "However, the Whisper of Sympathetic Consideration tells me: 'Set the old boy loose and let the law look after itself.' "

From his apparently depthless sack, the Mad Robber produced a couple of iron bars and a wedge. He and Jen succeeded in cracking the seal and prying open the cangue. Mafoo, observing their efforts, threw up his hands.

"Not another old crock!" he moaned as Jen ordered him to bring food and drink for Master Shu, who had sat down in the middle of the road. "Remember that bird of ill omen, that wretched Fu! Please, no more stray geezers! Feed this one, yes, but send him on his way."

Master Shu evidently had no intention of moving from the spot. He wolfed down the victuals that Mafoo brought and seemed to regain a little strength even as Jen watched.

"I feel light as a feather." Master Shu licked his

cracked lips and stretched his neck, which had been rubbed raw. "I had almost forgotten what it was like to be without this collar. How long did I wear it? A year? More? I have lost track of time. Magistrate Fat-choy sentenced me to the cangue for the rest of my life. Surely, he never expected me to survive this long."

"Fat-choy condemned you?" Jen broke in. "That overblown toad?"

"Yes, the magistrate of Feng-sia," Master Shu said. "I am a poet by occupation, and some of my verses offended Honorable Fat-choy—as, indeed, I hoped they would. Nevertheless, I must admit that he chose a most emphatic way of expressing his critical opinion. Your reference to an overblown toad leads me to believe you know him."

Mention of Fat-choy made Jen's back smart again. He ruefully told Master Shu what the official had done, as well as everything else that had happened since leaving the palace.

"An admirable undertaking marred by regrettable incidents," Master Shu said sympathetically. "However, if you wish to reach T'ien-kuo, you must not continue on this road."

"Just as I thought." Mafoo beetled his brow at Moxa. "This idiot's taken us in the wrong direction."

"T'ien-kuo lies beyond the River Lo," Master Shu went on. "This road will eventually lead you to it, but it is long and very roundabout. From here, there is a much more direct way; also, much more difficult.

However, if you have strength to follow it, you will arrive sooner at your destination."

"I'm sure you'll be kind enough to explain how we find that path," Voyaging Moon said.

"I was about to do so," Master Shu said. "It is somewhat complicated, but if you listen carefully—"

"The Ear of Continual Attentiveness—" Moxa began.

"Never mind that." Mafoo then quickly whispered to Jen, "Be sensible. How can we be sure he knows what he's talking about? He's a poet, isn't he?"

"You are quite right in raising such a question," said Master Shu, whose long punishment in the cangue had not damaged his hearing. "However, I assure you I am competent to speak of T'ien-kuo."

"You've been there?" said Voyaging Moon.

"Indeed, I have," Master Shu said. "It is a remarkable kingdom. I have seen it for myself. In a manner of speaking. That is to say, I have dreamed of it."

"What?" cried Mafoo. "Idiot! You've only been there in your dreams and you expect us to believe—"

"Poets are seldom believed," Master Shu said, "but I can tell you that my dreams are very clear, precise, and exact. You can rely on them far more than on maps and geographical treatises."

Mafoo clapped his hands to his head. "Young Lord, send him off. He's worse than Moxa."

"Do we have better information?" Jen said. "Master Hu told me once that a dream can be as useful as a fact."

"Yes, especially in the case of T'ien-kuo," Master Shu said.

"If you're sure you know the way," Jen said, after some long moments of thought, "will you guide us?"

"I am not at all certain I have the strength to venture so far," Master Shu said. "On the other hand, if you insist, how can I refuse?"

"You can if you try," Mafoo said to him. To Jen, he muttered, "First, you put yourself in the hands of a lunatic robber; now, another old crock, and a poet on top of it. Your trusting nature will be your ruination. And," he added, "mine as well."

◆　◆　◆　◆　◆

Is Mafoo right? Has our hero made yet another mistake? How reliable is Master Shu? These questions require time to find their answers, so it will be necessary to go on to the next chapter.

13

· *Guidance of Master Shu* ·
· *Affairs of the feet and stomach* ·
· *Affairs of the heart* ·

MAFOO EYED MASTER SHU with the same enthusiasm he would have given a ten-day-old carp. Jen had no misgivings. He willingly followed the poet's instructions, turning off the road and onto a track leading across open countryside. Voyaging Moon urged Master Shu to ride in the cart. He shook his head, declaring that he had been tramping so long he would be uncomfortable doing otherwise.

"My feet will outlast any horse's hooves." Master Shu displayed his soles, covered with thick, scarred calluses, tougher than leather. "By the time we reach the River Lo," he added, "yours will be the same."

"Now, there's something to look forward to. I can hardly wait," Mafoo remarked. However, seeing no choice in the matter, he trudged beside Moxa, who continued insisting that he had not misguided them.

Despite his rising spirits, three questions troubled Jen. As the day wore on, he ventured to speak of them to Master Shu.

"About the gifts for Yuan-ming," Jen said. "As I told you, Master Wu chose six and I've lost two. Dare I now present only four? It seems a small number for such a great king."

"For one thing," Master Shu replied, "as you described the circumstances, I would not say that you lost them. You did what seemed altogether reasonable. Certainly, as far as the sword is concerned, had you not let that ruffian take it you would not be alive at this moment to make the journey.

"For another, will Yuan-ming know or care how many gifts you started out with? The important thing is that you will not arrive empty-handed. Besides, along the way, you may find other gifts even more valuable."

Master Shu's words reassured Jen to some extent. He was satisfied that he still had sufficient offerings. Now he brought up another question troubling him as much.

"My royal warrant is gone. How can I prove who I am? You believed me, but Fat-choy didn't. Why should Yuan-ming take my word? I'll be a stranger to him—not a very princely looking one, at that. Will he even admit me to his presence?

"Once we reach the capital," Jen continued, "should I first write him a petition explaining what happened?"

"That's a reasonable thought," Voyaging Moon said. "It might be wiser than just walking up to the palace and trying to persuade the guards to let you in."

"Do you believe so?" Master Shu said. "Let me tell you the tale of Foolish Yang and the shoes.

"Deciding to buy a new pair of shoes, Foolish Yang measured his feet and wrote the figures on a piece of paper. Hurrying to the seller of shoes, he requested a pair matching the dimensions he had noted down. The merchant found such a pair and, offering them to Yang, urged him to try them on.

"Yang did so, then burst out unhappily: 'They pinch my toes! They rub my heels! Too short in length, too narrow in width. They fit me not at all!'

" 'Let me see that paper,' said the shoe seller. 'Now, look here, Honorable Yang, they tally exactly with these measurements.'

"Yang scratched his head and pondered a while. 'You are right,' he said at last. 'Obviously, I made a mistake when I wrote out the figures. Very well, there is nothing else for it. I must go back home and measure my feet again.'

"By the same token," Master Shu said, "to which will Yuan-ming give more belief: a scrap of paper, or the individual who wrote it? My dear young man, Yuan-ming is wise enough. He will know you for what you are."

Again, Jen felt reassured. One last question troubled him, and most deeply of all.

"My honored father wishes me to learn how Yuan-ming governs his kingdom," Jen said. "It did not occur to me at the time, but now I realize it means I'll have to study every one of his laws and precepts, his regulations, ordinances, decrees, analects—how shall I do this? I wasn't educated to be a scholar or official. I understand nothing of these things."

"You must know nothing before you can learn something, and be empty before you can be filled. Is not the emptiness of the bowl what makes it useful? As for laws, a parrot can repeat them word for word. Their spirit is something else again. As for governing, one must first be lowest before being highest. The pot must be broken before it can be mended—"

Master Shu left off, for Mafoo was calling to them. In the course of their conversation, Jen and the old poet had lagged behind. Running to catch up, Jen saw that Mafoo had halted at the edge of a steep cliff.

"Fine guide!" Mafoo exclaimed as Master Shu approached. "If I hadn't my wits about me, I'd have gone tumbling over, horse, cart, and all."

"Dear me, dear me," Master Shu said, "that would have been regrettable, especially for the horse. Very well, unhitch him and let him go his way."

"What?" cried Mafoo. "What are you saying?"

"We can hardly take a horse and cart," Master Shu replied. "We shall have difficulty enough climbing down with sacks of provisions on our backs."

"He's right," said Voyaging Moon, looking into the valley. "Too steep. There's no path at all."

"Master Shu," Jen demanded, alarmed. "Where have you led us?"

"Where you must go," said Master Shu.

Now followed a conversation between Mafoo and Master Shu. It consisted, for the most part, of Master Shu saying nothing, while Mafoo vigorously suggested that Master Shu was a greater lunatic than Moxa if he expected them to give up their only transportation and much of their food.

"He is very persuasive," Master Shu said to Jen when Mafoo ran out of breath, "and he has your best interests at heart. The problem is: Either you trust me or you do not."

Jen stepped to the girl's side and studied the downward slope. As Voyaging Moon had told him, it was not possible to take the horse and cart.

"I have to trust him," Jen said finally. "I don't know what else to do." He took Voyaging Moon's hand. "If I follow him, will you come with me?"

"Did you think I wouldn't?" Voyaging Moon said.

Jen turned to Moxa. "I'm going with Master Shu. I can't ask you to do the same. You'd do better to go back to robbery—if you can ever find a likely candidate, that is."

"Never!" cried Moxa, flinging himself at Jen's feet. "The Heart of Eternal Devotion, the Hand of Enthusiastic Obedience—"

"Mafoo," Jen said, disentangling himself from the devoted clutches of the Mad Robber, "my good Mafoo, best of faithful servants, you are wiser than I am, but I can only do what seems good to me. Go safely to Ch'ang-an. Tell my father I ordered you to do so."

"Young Lord," Mafoo said, "if you're set on doing something as foolish as this, all the more reason for me to keep an eye on you."

With that, Mafoo stumped to the cart and set about unhitching the horse. Master Shu trotted after him as the animal, glad to be relieved of its burden, tossed its head and kicked up its heels. The old man patted the horse's neck.

"Get along with you," Master Shu said. "You are free. Go about your business."

"Oh, no!" Mafoo puffed out his cheeks. "The old boy talks to horses?"

Shouldering as many sacks of food as they could, the travelers followed Master Shu, who had begun scrambling down as nimbly as a monkey. The old man was quicker and more surefooted than Jen could have imagined; nevertheless, it was late afternoon by the time they reached the floor of the dry gorge. Jen glanced at the cliffs towering high above.

"I'm wondering," he said to Master Shu, "how we're going to climb up on the way back."

"Do not concern yourself," Master Shu said

brightly, turning a sharp eye on Jen. An odd note came into his voice as he added, "You will not set foot here again."

In the days and weeks that followed, Jen wondered if he had, in fact, done well to follow Master Shu. The old poet had warned of difficulties and had not exaggerated. This stretch of the valley, he explained, had long ago been the bed of a mighty river. The earth had rumbled and shattered, the river vanished; boulders greater than the whole Celestial Palace had been flung up as if no more than pebbles. Astonishingly, Master Shu easily clambered up them while Jen and the others strained and sweated to keep pace with him. Sometimes they lost sight of the old man, only to find him perched on the highest peak of a stone slab, waving his staff and beckoning to them.

In time, however, they grew hardened to the rugged course Master Shu had set, and the old man no longer outdistanced them. In the matter of their feet, Master Shu's prediction had been correct. Jen ceased to be aware of the sharp stones; Voyaging Moon, though accustomed to going unshod, saw that her soles had toughened still more. Moxa's boots had long since been torn to shreds, but he loped along, agile as a cat, making long-legged leaps from one rocky outcrop to another.

The summer sun blistered their faces and parched their throats. Yet, when their mouths had so dried that even Mafoo could barely grumble, Master Shu found some rivulet or trickle of water. As for food, by Jen's calculations it should have long since run out. Nevertheless, the apparently empty sacks of provisions always held yet another handful of rice or millet cakes. What disappeared was Mafoo's paunch.

"Look at me," he groaned. "Now my belt's too long by half. Keep on like this and I'll be thinner than a shadow."

"I don't think he minds all that much," Voyaging Moon whispered to Jen, glimpsing Mafoo furtively admiring his new leanness. "Even so, I have to agree with him."

Soon after, an eagle flew overhead, gripping a wriggling fish in its talons. Next moment, it let go of the fish, which dropped at the feet of Master Shu.

"Marvelous!" cried Mafoo. "Here's our dinner falling from the sky! Hold on there, old fellow, what are you doing?" he added as Master Shu bent down to put his ear close to the fish and seemed to strike up an earnest conversation.

"Begging his forgiveness and asking if he objects to our eating him," replied Master Shu. "That is only common courtesy. He agrees this time, but tells me not to make a habit of it."

Mafoo threw up his hands. "First he talks to horses, now he talks to fish." He cocked an eye at Master Shu. "Enough of your nonsense. How do you know what he says? You're not a fish."

"Nor are you Master Shu," replied the poet, smiling. "How do you know that I do not know?"

With Mafoo trying to puzzle out Master Shu's logic, the travelers enjoyed their best meal since entering the gorge.

That night, as she had always done, Voyaging Moon played the flute. Its music, in these bleak surroundings, had never sounded sweeter. When she finished and the last echoes died away, Master Shu happily announced that the most difficult part of their journey now lay behind them; within a day, they would reach the T'ung Pass, and from there he foresaw less than a week of easy travel to the banks of the Lo.

The old man's news should have cheered Jen as much as it did Moxa and Mafoo. Strangely, the closer he drew to his destination the more reluctant he became to end his journey. Even if Yuan-ming accepted him, Jen could not guess how long he might be obliged to remain. Weeks, probably months of study lay ahead before he started homeward again. Another question concerned him still more. While the others settled into sleep, he spoke of it to Voyaging Moon.

"If the end of my journey also means parting from you," Jen said, "I—then I think I will have journeyed uselessly. Whatever else I might gain, I will have lost something greater. Will you stay with me in T'ien-kuo? Yuan-ming surely will make a place for all of us."

"If I do?" Voyaging Moon quietly replied. "And afterward?"

"Come back with me to Ch'ang-an," Jen said, taking her hand.

"Does the Celestial Palace require a flute girl?" Her voice was light as her teasing laughter.

"No, it doesn't." Jen smiled at her. "I do."

"Aren't there enough musicians in the Celestial Palace?" Voyaging Moon said. "Why should the Young Lord Prince wish another?"

"There's no Young Lord Prince," Jen said. "Between us, there's no Jen Shao-yeh. Only myself. And yourself."

"That's easy to say, sitting on a pile of rocks in the middle of nowhere," Voyaging Moon replied. "Once you're in the palace again——"

"You have my promise as well as my heart," Jen said. "I have no betrothal token. What I would offer you is a gift that must be given up: this flute. Even so, carry it now as if it were your own. If Yuan-ming is as gracious as Master Wu claimed, he'll understand that it is yours more truly than it can be his."

Voyaging Moon nodded and picked up the instrument she had set aside. "Whether I must part with it or not, you, too, have my promise——"

A cry from Master Shu made Voyaging Moon break off. The old man suddenly sat bolt upright, muttering wildly. As Jen and Voyaging Moon hurried to his side, he rubbed his eyes and blinked around.

"Dear me, dear me," he murmured, "have I been dreaming? I hope so. Sometimes it is difficult to be sure. There was another poet, once, who dreamed he was a butterfly. When he woke, he could not decide whether he was a poet dreaming he was a butterfly or a butterfly dreaming he was a poet. No matter, either way it is only a dream."

Master Shu would say no more of what had disturbed him, and he beamed with delight when Jen and Voyaging Moon told him of their promises to one another. By this time, Mafoo and Moxa had awakened, and the news had to be repeated; it was met with so many joyous congratulations and blessings from the two of them that Master Shu at last had to urge them to leave off.

"That should be ample happiness for one day," he said. "Keep a little stored away. It might be needed."

◆　◆　◆　◆　◆

Marvelous turn of events! What could be happier? Those who are content to end the tale here with two young lovers need go no further. Those curious to learn more of the journey must read the next chapter.

14

• Happiness of Jen •
• Sadness of Master Shu •
• Ferryboat at the River Lo •

MASTER SHU, NEXT DAY, led the travelers through the T'ung Pass. Here, the rock-strewn course veered away. Jen found himself in the greenest woodlands and meadows he had ever seen. Along the forest track, yellow and crimson wildflowers turned the air fragrant. Birds of every color flew overhead or perched, singing, amid the trees. Monkeys skittered along the branches and chattered at the human intruders. Voyaging Moon laughed in delight as a gazelle daintily trotted across the path and halted a moment to glance at her before vanishing into the foliage.

Jen would have gladly lingered. He had never been happier. Hand in hand with Voyaging Moon, smiling whenever their eyes met, his loss of the sword and saddle and his beating by Fat-choy's retainers no longer seemed important.

"Mafoo once complained about Master Fu," Jen said to her. "If he hadn't fallen into the river, I wouldn't have fished him out and taken him with us. If I hadn't done that, I wouldn't have gone to Kwan-tzu. If I hadn't gone to Kwan-tzu, we wouldn't have met. Blame Master Fu? I should thank him."

As for Mafoo's usual complaints, they stopped altogether. Even more surprising, he no longer grumbled about Moxa and in fact had come to be on friendly terms with the Mad Robber. One day, when the travelers were obliged to ford a deep stream, Mafoo unhappily eyed the swift current and admitted he could not swim.

"Hop on the Shoulders of Reliable Support," Moxa said. "You're lighter than you used to be."

With Mafoo clinging uneasily to his back, Moxa plunged into the water up to his nose. Once across, when Mafoo thanked him, Moxa shook his ropy hair and grinned happily.

"Glad to oblige," Moxa said, adding, "I needed your weight to keep me from floating away. I forgot to mention: I can't swim, either."

Instead of berating him, Moxa burst out laughing; and the two of them raced on ahead, capering like a pair of schoolboys.

Only Master Shu seemed low-spirited. His steps had slowed, he leaned more heavily on his staff. Often, as they made their way through the woodlands, Voyaging Moon played the flute she now carried, but its music brought only shadows to the old poet's furrowed face.

Two days later, they left the forest track to follow a hard-packed roadway. Here, they saw other travelers, merchants in carriages or sedan chairs, farmers with ox carts and wheelbarrows of produce on their way to Chen-yeh, the district capital close to the banks of the Lo. Mafoo licked his lips at the prospect of dumpling houses, but Master Shu announced that they would turn away from the town and go farther upriver, where they would attract less attention. He recalled a ferryman there who would row them across.

The old man urged them to make haste. For some while, Master Shu had been sniffing the air and casting uneasy glances at the gathering clouds. The closer they drew to the river, the darker grew the sky. Late that afternoon, by the time they sighted the ferryman's hut, the first raindrops had begun to fall.

Of the ferryman himself, there was no sign. Mafoo and Moxa went off to find him, while Jen and Voyaging Moon made their way to the water's edge. The river was broader than Jen had envisioned, and he could barely make out the green banks of the farther shore.

Master Shu pointed with his staff. "Once across, you must yet go many leagues to Ch'ung-chao. I had hoped I might guide you all the way."

"What do you mean?" Jen replied. "Of course you will. Why wouldn't you?"

Master Shu did not answer. Before Jen could question him further, Mafoo and Moxa were back; with them was the ferryman, shaking his head and pointing at the lowering sky.

"He's worried about a storm. Once the rain starts, the fellow claims it could last for days," Mafoo said. He added brightly, "Nothing else for it. We'll have to go to Chen-yeh and put up with the hardships of an inn, with all those hot meals and soft beds."

"I'm bound to find a client or two there," Moxa said. "We'll manage nicely."

"A few more days won't matter," Voyaging Moon said, while Master Shu remained silent, offering no opinion.

Jen hesitated. Delay would make little difference. Yet, with the river before him, his impatience grew. He wished to be across and on the way to T'ien-kuo. He questioned the ferryman, who admitted he could likely reach the farther shore before the storm broke. The return was what troubled him. He might, he protested, be stranded on the opposite bank who knew how long, away from wife and children, soaked to the skin, catching a cold into the bargain.

"Aha!" cried Moxa. "The Nose of Thoughtful Inhalations smells a question of money. Well, then, cash cures all complaints." Delving into his sack, he produced a handful of silver coins and a string of coppers, and the sum, indeed, outweighed the ferryman's reluctance.

"Settled, then," said Jen. "We'll cross now."

The ferryman urged the travelers to board immediately. Voyaging Moon, tucking the flute in her jacket, sprang lightly into the boat. Jen helped Master Shu to a place astern, between Mafoo and Moxa. The ferryman bent to his oars, the craft slid into the current.

The wind had freshened; the waters of the Lo turned choppy. Well before the boat reached midstream, the waves began snatching at it. Despite his efforts, the ferryman could not hold to his course. The current bore the craft farther downriver, well away from the little dock on the opposite shore.

Now the sky had turned black, and the rain began in earnest, pouring down in blinding sheets. The wind rose to a screaming gale. The boat pitched and spun like a leaf on the tide.

"Row back! Row back!" Mafoo cried, gripping the side of the boat, while Moxa crouched beside Master Shu.

"No!" Jen shouted, throwing his arms around Voyaging Moon. "That's as dangerous. Keep on. If the wind slackens—"

The ferryman could obey neither command. As he hauled with all his might at the oars, one of them snapped, and he tumbled backward. The helpless craft slewed around in the clutches of tide and gale.

The boat plunged into the trough of the waves,

then suddenly flung upward, lurched sideways, and shuddered an instant before it capsized.

The shock tore Voyaging Moon from Jen's arms. Water closed over his head. He fought his way to the surface again. Lightning like clawing fingers ripped the sky. In flash after flash, he glimpsed Mafoo and Moxa floundering in the tide, the ferryman trying desperately to keep afloat. Master Shu had vanished, his staff tossed like a straw on the waves.

Jen, in that moment, saw Voyaging Moon struggling against the current. He shouted to her, but the wind bore away his words. Then she caught sight of him and stretched out her hands. He swam toward her. The shattered boat spun between them. A broken timber struck him full force. Her face was the last thing he would remember.

· · · · ·

Jen is snatched from his beloved, his friends swept away in the tide and scattered to the winds. However, before returning to our hero and his fate, we must now follow along with Voyaging Moon. The tale of her own journey is told in the next chapter.

15

· *The Tale of the Singing Flute* ·

A MAN CALLED HONG was innkeeper of the Golden Grasshopper in the town of Chen-yeh. This fellow Hong had a quick eye for profit and a deaf ear for whatever did not work to his advantage. He gave nothing without getting more in return. No one ever bettered him in a bargain. When a terrible storm forced travelers to seek refuge at his inn, Hong doubled his prices for food and lodging, delighted that the misfortunes of others turned into a benefit for himself.

It was at this time, some days after the storm had

passed, that a young girl came to the kitchen door and politely asked for food. Her face was bruised, her garments were torn and weather-stained. Even so, she did not have the air of one accustomed to begging. The cook would gladly have given her a handful of leftovers, but Hong happened to come into the kitchen at that moment. When he saw what the cook was about to do, Hong shouted angrily at him and pushed him aside.

"Do you mean to bankrupt me?" he cried. "Your business is cooking food, not giving it away." He turned to the girl. "Be off. You'll get nothing for nothing here."

The girl did not move, but looked squarely at Hong. She was none other than Voyaging Moon. The gale that had swept away Jen and the others had flung her amid the reeds and cattails of a little backwater. Battered, half-drowned, she opened her eyes to find herself alone, the flute clutched tightly in her hand. For days afterward, she searched along the riverbank from dawn to dusk, even through most of the nights. She questioned children playing along the shore, women washing clothes in the shallows, and everyone who crossed her path. No one, they told her sadly, could have survived such a tempest on the river. What kept her heart from breaking then and there was her certainty that since she was alive, so must the others be.

At last, driven by hunger and exhaustion, she came to Chen-yeh and the Golden Grasshopper. Once she had eaten a little and regained strength, she determined to search yet again, to comb both banks of the Lo from source to mouth if need be. The innkeeper's refusal did not discourage her in the least.

"Nothing for nothing?" Voyaging Moon said. "That's a fair exchange. What of something for something? My work for your food."

Hong thought this over for a few moments. His inn was crowded, his servants hardly able to keep up with their tasks, his guests already complaining and threatening to leave if conditions did not get better. He badly needed another pair of willing hands, and he quickly calculated the girl's labor would be worth far more than what she ate. Of that, he would make sure.

"Agreed," Hong said, with a show of reluctance, "but only because I have a generous heart. You can have what you scrape out of those pots and pans and not a mouthful more. For the rest, you'll do as you're told, no shirking, no laziness. Even at that, I'm cheating myself. But I can't help it, that's how I am."

"Generosity must be a painful affliction," Voyaging Moon sympathized. "I hope you don't suffer too much from it."

All that day, Voyaging Moon did every task that Hong demanded, scrubbing, sweeping, fetching water, hauling charcoal, with never a word of complaint. The cook secretly made sure the girl was fed with more than pot scrapings, and he prepared her a pallet of straw in the kitchen corner.

At nightfall, when Voyaging Moon finished her work, she did not rest. A hopeful thought had come to her mind. She left the kitchen and climbed to the roof of the inn.

There, perched cross-legged on the tiles, she put the flute to her lips and played a soaring melody, praying that somehow Jen would hear it wherever he might be and that the music would bring him to her.

As she played, her heart followed the notes shimmering like stars in the dark sky. The voice of the flute sang of love, longing, and hope. Indeed, the instrument seemed to have its own spirit that spoke wordlessly but clearly, as if playing of itself, its tone more beautiful than it had ever been.

Voyaging Moon stopped. She was not alone. The music, meant for Jen, had drawn other listeners. Guests had come out of their chambers, tradesmen from their shops, passersby had halted in the street below. As Voyaging Moon put aside her instrument, cries of disappointment rose from the crowd, and they pleaded for her to continue.

The innkeeper had hurried from his counting room to learn the cause of the commotion outside.

"Come down," he shouted when he saw Voyaging Moon and her flute. "You should be scrubbing pots for your keep, not amusing yourself on my valuable time. You'd best put a broom in your hand instead of that wooden whistle."

At this, the crowd around Hong protested loudly,

insisting on the girl playing again. A few even threatened to give Hong a good beating if he forbade her to do so. Many more, however, pressed money into his hands, urging him to reward such a marvelous musician and induce her to keep on. The bewildered innkeeper had wits enough to pop the cash into his purse. Though he had no ear for music, he heard coins clinking merrily enough; and, by the time Voyaging Moon climbed from the roof, Hong's vinegar frown was transformed into a honeyed smile.

"My dear young lady," Hong said, "if I spoke harshly it was only because I feared for your safety. You could have fallen and harmed yourself. Step inside, night air is bad for the lungs. If only you had told me you had such a valuable skill! Have you eaten well today? Come along, come along," he added, taking Voyaging Moon's arm and drawing her inside.

The guests, along with a number of passersby, followed. All begged to hear more of her music. Hong made a place for Voyaging Moon in the middle of the eating room, called for food and drink to be served to her; then, rubbing his hands, he asked her to take up the flute again.

"Surely you won't deny these good folk the pleasure of your music," Hong said. "Look around you, lovely lady, and see how many have come to hear."

Though Voyaging Moon's grief had burdened her heart, it had not dulled her wits. She saw that Hong had gone to each one in the room, demanding more cash. His purse was already full to bursting. It came quickly to her mind that a share of Hong's profit would allow her to hire a riverboat, buy provisions, and employ helpers in her search for Jen.

"I won't deny anyone the pleasure of my music," she replied sweetly, "and you, Master Hong, won't deny me payment for it. As you yourself told me: nothing for nothing."

Hong sputtered and protested, but the guests had grown impatient, threatening to leave and demanding their money back. So, Hong fished into his purse and produced a couple of coins.

"Why, Master Hong, what of your generous heart?" Voyaging Moon said. "Not to mention the weight of your purse. It seems to me we can strike a better bargain. Equal portions should be a reasonable division. No, no, you're right, that won't do at all," she added, as Hong squealed indignantly. "Much better to make it three coins out of ten. That is, three for you and seven for me."

Hong shook his fists and tore his hair, claiming that Voyaging Moon would ruin him.

"How can that be?" Voyaging Moon said. "Since it cost you nothing to begin with, what you gain is pure profit. Furthermore, if I refuse to play, you'll gain nothing at all."

No matter how the innkeeper groaned and wrung his hands, Voyaging Moon held to her offer. Finally, Hong grudgingly accepted. Voyaging Moon then played for the assembled audience, so charmingly and graciously that Hong was able to extract still more cash from them as well as from new arrivals. At the end of the evening, Voyaging Moon required the innkeeper to spread all the coins on a table, holding nothing back, and she herself made the division. Even with his three coins out of ten, Hong reckoned on fat profits in his future.

"I should also mention," Voyaging Moon said, "that I'd play much better if I slept in my own chamber instead of a straw mat in the kitchen."

Hong ground his teeth but finally had to agree. Voyaging Moon tucked her earnings into her jacket and retired to the room Hong reluctantly provided. Next evening, she played again before an even larger audience, to the increasing joy of the innkeeper. She did likewise the following evening. Nevertheless, when she had finished performing, she still climbed to the roof and poured out her music to the night sky, ever hopeful it would reach the ears of her beloved.

By the end of the week, Voyaging Moon calculated that she had earned enough to continue her search better outfitted than before. She announced to the innkeeper that she would depart the following morning. Hong was furious at the thought of losing future profits. Voyaging Moon, however, told him flatly that she would play no longer and in no way could he force her to do so.

"If you try," she warned, "I'll play so badly it will

drive every guest from your inn and you'll be worse off than ever."

Hong could not browbeat her into changing her mind. Realizing she was no longer of use to him, he quickly shaped a plan. "The wench thinks she's had the better of me? That remains to be seen."

Hong set his plan in motion without an instant's delay. That very night, he struck up a conversation with a merchant who had just arrived and planned to leave early next morning.

"One of my bondmaids has taken advantage of my good nature," Hong told the merchant. "She's turned slack and impudent and I'd like to be rid of her. I haven't the heart to throw her out into the street. I'll sell her to you at a bargain price if I'm sure you'll give her a good home. She may need a stricter hand than mine. I've been too soft with her; that's my nature. But, if you pay no heed to the lies and wild tales she tells, and let her know who's master, she'll be obedient enough. She can even tootle a few notes on the flute, but I won't ask extra for that. One thing I do want," he added, "is that jacket she wears. I loaned it to her and must have it back."

Considering that his wife had been plaguing him to buy a bondmaid, the merchant gladly paid out the low price Hong demanded. Before dawn the next day, they went to Voyaging Moon's chamber. Hong had forewarned the merchant that the girl was so devoted to him that she would resist every effort to take her away;

therefore, the innkeeper provided some lengths of rope at no added charge.

Voyaging Moon was already awake and dressed when the two burst in. Though taken unawares, she kicked and bit and fought with all her strength. But they overpowered her. Hong tore away the jacket, where she had hidden her money. Voyaging Moon found herself bound and gagged, hauled down to the stable, and thrown into the merchant's carriage along with her flute. Captive, robbed of her earnings, she was borne southward, far from the River Lo where she had planned to search.

For all that, she kept a brave heart. Her determination only strengthened. Therefore, during the days that followed, instead of raging and struggling, she cleverly made a show of docility. The merchant felt confident enough to remove her gag. She told him she was glad to be free of Hong—which was quite true. She gathered that the merchant lived in Chai-sang, the capital of the northern province. She resolved to escape before they reached that city.

During the journey, the merchant lodged Voyaging Moon in stables of roadside inns where they halted at each day's end. Before retiring, he made sure the girl was securely tied for the night. One evening, as he was about to leave the stable for his chamber, Voyaging Moon called him back.

"Now that we're far from Master Hong," she said, "I can tell you this. He cheated you. You brought my flute along, didn't you? Yes, well, what he didn't tell you is that it's a remarkable instrument. When played, you'd be amazed at what it does."

Voyaging Moon would explain no further. The merchant, his curiosity roused, took the flute from the carriage. He examined it, finding nothing extraordinary. Voyaging Moon urged him to blow into it. When he did so, however, he produced nothing but squeaks and whistles.

"Let me show you how," Voyaging Moon said. "Untie my hands so I can hold it properly."

The merchant did as she asked, then sat down in a corner of the stable and watched her closely. Hoping and praying her plan would succeed, Voyaging Moon put the flute to her lips. Hardly breathing, she played the softest, gentlest melody. The flute whispered and murmured as if its spirit answered her wishes.

"Remarkable, indeed," the merchant said in a hushed voice. "Why, it seems the same lullaby my mother sang to me when I was an infant. I've heard nothing like it these many years." He brushed away a tear. "Keep on, keep on, I beg you."

The merchant closed his eyes and blissfully smiled. Within moments, his head nodded and dropped to his breast. Blowing out his lips, toying with his fingers, he soon snored and gurgled happily away.

Voyaging Moon tucked the flute into her shirt. "You don't mind if I borrow your horse, do you?" Receiving no contrary answer, she quickly unhitched the animal. Before climbing astride, she patted the slumbering merchant on the head.

"Sweet dreams," said Voyaging Moon.

Though it was not the largest of towns, Nang-pei boasted the finest theater in the province. Traveling companies of tumblers, jugglers, singers, and dancers went out of their way to stop there. The folk of Nang-pei always welcomed these performers. That autumn, however, the one who drew their warmest applause, their loudest cheers, and their delighted devotion was a girl who charmed them with the music of her flute. She could not set foot in the streets without admirers crowding around her. Young swains, love-smitten, sent her jewels, necklaces, and bracelets, along with flowers and heartrending notes begging her hand in marriage. But the girl graciously declined all such offerings. Rumor had it that she was richer than any of her would-be suitors.

When not performing, she kept mainly to herself in chambers above the theater. Unlike her colleagues, she did not bedeck herself in bright robes, fanciful headdresses, and other garish finery. On stage, she wore a coarse cotton shirt and trousers. This peasant simplicity endeared her all the more to her devoted audiences. Also, she had the strange custom, each night, of climbing to the rooftop and, alone, playing melodies still more beautiful than those she played in public. This odd habit only enraptured her listeners.

Because of a certain air of mystery about her, and because she was never seen in public eating rooms, teahouses, or taverns, the townsfolk affectionately called her Lady Shadow Behind a Screen.

She was, in fact, Voyaging Moon. All this had come about after she had galloped off leaving the merchant sleeping soundly. Heading northward again, she happened to fall in with a troupe of dancers and jugglers on their way to Nang-pei. Seeing that she carried a flute, they persuaded her to play and were so enchanted they urged her to join them. At first, she refused. She intended to continue to the River Lo. This, she was told, would be extremely dangerous, if not altogether impossible.

As one of the jugglers explained, a powerful warlord was ravaging the countryside, defeating every army sent against him. He already held sway in many districts. His troops showed no regard or mercy for innocent folk caught between the lines of these fierce battles. It was said he had once been a bandit. Now, he called himself the Yellow Scarf King.

Voyaging Moon remembered all too well the brutality of Natha. Impatient though she was to continue northward, she could not risk falling into his clutches again. For the moment, she reluctantly had to admit, the sensible course was to heed the troupe's warning and follow their advice. And so she went with them to Nang-pei.

There, the theater director was as openhanded as

Hong had been tightfisted. Hearing her play, he promised a handsome share of his profits and was better than his word. Her fame and fortune grew. Voyaging Moon—or, Lady Shadow Behind a Screen—was able to commission the best craftsmen to build her a carriage, so spacious and well-appointed that she could live in it as comfortably as in a chamber. She bought six fine horses and began to lay in a store of provisions, hoping the fighting would subside and she might leave Nang-pei before winter.

Meantime, she played her flute alone each night on the rooftop, her thoughts ever turning to Jen. Had he continued to T'ien-kuo? Had he found Mafoo or Moxa? Was he still alive? Of that, she never permitted herself to doubt.

"If he has gone," she told herself, "he will come back. If he is searching for me, he will find me."

• • • • •

Are Voyaging Moon's hopes justified? While she, by accident, has gained fame and fortune, what has become of her beloved Jen? To find out, leave Voyaging Moon in Nang-pei and read the next chapter.

16

• What is fished out of the river •
• What is told to Jen •
• What is to be decided •

HE LAY ON A PILE OF STRAW. Sunlight streamed through a narrow doorway. A gray-haired woman bent over him. A man's weathered face peered down.

"Where are they?" Jen tried to sit up. He was in the corner of a hut. Nets hung from the low ceiling. His head pounded as if the storm filled it. He could scarcely bring his eyes to focus. "Where—?"

"Safe." The woman smiled. "I'll fetch them."

"Fished out along with you," the man added. "Wet, but undamaged."

Jen gave a joyous cry. His last memory was the face of Voyaging Moon, her hands outstretched, struggling in the tide. The storm was over. They had lived through it.

The woman was back. She held out a bundle. "See. We kept your goods carefully."

"No!" Jen burst out. "Not these! My friends—"

"No others," the fisherman said. "You were alone. More than half-drowned, and with a broken head, too."

"They must be nearby. Washed ashore with me." The hut spun before Jen's eyes. "We were all together, crossing the river yesterday. The boat foundered—"

The fisherman and his wife exchanged glances. The woman spoke gently. "The storm passed a week and more ago. You've lain here since then. We feared you'd never come back to your senses. Rest. Take food now."

"A week?" Jen stared around wildly. "Where is this? We crossed above Chen-yeh—"

"Chen-yeh?" The fisherman raised his eyebrows. "You're leagues from there. The river carried you far downstream. Be glad you're alive."

"My friends are alive, too. They must be."

The fisherman was about to speak. His wife gestured to him. "Let him believe so, if that will help him," she murmured.

"I'll find them." Jen lurched to his feet. His legs buckled under him. He fell back onto the straw. He had heard the woman's words. "Yes, they are alive," he said. "I believe it. I know it." He wondered if he was telling himself the truth.

Two days passed before Jen could stand unaided, and another day before he could walk. Even then, he was light-headed, his steps uncertain. The fisherman and his wife urged him to wait until he had his full strength again.

"Young man," the fisherman said, "who you are and what your business may be is no affair of ours. You don't strike me as a murderer or a thief. If you've run afoul of the law in some way—there's plenty like you in the kingdom, for His Majesty's officials deal out more injustice than otherwise. No matter, you stay with us, if you want, as long as you want."

Only then did Jen realize the couple had never asked his name, but tended him nonetheless. "I've not run afoul of any laws," he said. "I'm seeking to learn better ones."

"So I hope you do," the fisherman said, questioning him no further.

When Jen thanked the couple, telling them he must seek his friends, the fisherman and his wife shared what food they could spare to help him on his journey. Taking grateful leave of them, Jen set out following the river upstream. He thought to find the ferryman's hut. If the man had lived out the storm, he might know something of Voyaging Moon, Mafoo, Moxa, and Master Shu.

Meantime, trudging along the Lo, he questioned all

who lived near the riverbank. They treated him kindly, gave food when his supply ran out, and let him sleep under their roofs at night. But they could tell him nothing.

Despite that, his hope did not lessen. For there were times, when he lay restless and wakeful, half in a dream, it seemed that the voice of Voyaging Moon called out to him. He even imagined hearing the shimmering notes of the flute. This, he knew, was only a memory that both saddened and lifted his heart.

He came in sight of Chen-yeh by week's end. He did not skirt the town as he had planned. Rather, he found his steps drawn to crooked streets of dwellings and shops, hawkers of rags, of sweetmeats, of fighting crickets. A seller of birds, with bamboo cages stacked high beside him, cried his wares.

"Buy! Buy! All sweet singers. Sweet as the flute girl's melodies."

Jen stopped short. He had heard correctly, his ears had not deceived him. He ran to the bird seller. "What flute girl? What melodies?"

The man blinked at him. "You're a stranger in Chen-yeh, that's easy to guess. Flute girl? We've all heard and won't forget her. She used to play at the Golden Grasshopper, the inn of Master Hong."

"Where?" Jen's heart raced. The bird seller pointed up the street.

"A stranger for sure, if you don't know the Golden Grasshopper. There, to the right, past Phoenix Lane."

Jen set off running where the bird seller had indicated. In the courtyard of the inn, a man with the look
of the proprietor was berating a servant maid for laziness. Jen strode up to him.

"A girl who played the flute. She was here. I was
told so. Where is she now?"

"What's that to you?" Hong looked him up and
down. "Get out. I don't lodge beggars."

Jen took Hong by the shirt collar. "What it is to
me," he said between his teeth, "is this: I asked you a
question. I'll have an answer."

Hong choked, his eyes bulged as he tried to shake
free of Jen's grip. "Madman! Hands off! I'll call the law
on you. All right, let go," he gasped. "She's gone. Long
gone."

Jen set the innkeeper down hard on his heels. Puffing and scowling, Hong rubbed his neck. "Lunatic
devil," he muttered. He cocked an eye at Jen. "Yes. She
was here and she left. Good riddance to her."

"Her name?"

"How should I know? She worked in my kitchen. I
don't concern myself with scullery maids. Peasant girl,
from the look of her," he quickly added, backing away
as Jen stepped closer. "Yes, she played the flute a few
times. I paid her well for it, the ungrateful wench."

"Then?"

"Gone, I told you," Hong flung at him. "Who the
devil are you? What do you care? Aha—your little
sweetheart, eh?" A look of sly malice crept into the

innkeeper's eyes. "So that's your interest, is it? Well, my handsome fellow, I can tell you a little something else about her. Oh, she's gone, yes," Hong added. He grinned at Jen. "But not alone—if you take my meaning."

"What are you saying?" Jen demanded. "Who was with her?"

"Not a wretch like you," Hong said. "I'm a tender-hearted man, I wanted to spare your feelings. But why should I? She had eyes for one of my guests, with more in his purse than you have. The pair of them ran off together. And there you have it. The way of the world."

Hong gave Jen a scornful glance, turned on his heel, and hurried away, leaving Jen staring after him.

By the time Jen found words, Hong had disappeared. Jen stood, head reeling as if he had been struck in the face. He started after the innkeeper. As he did, one of the grooms loitering close by beckoned to him. Still trying to swallow what Hong had said, Jen stepped toward the man.

"Too bad you didn't choke that son of a turtle," the groom said under his breath. "I saw it all. Listen to me, lad. Hong's a liar as well as a cheat. The girl was here a while, true. How did she leave? I was in an empty stall that night. There was scuffling that woke me up. I saw Hong and one of his lodgers, the girl bound and gagged between them. A merchant of some sort, I don't know his name. They packed her into his carriage, and he drove off as fast as he could. Later, I heard the merchant went south, to Chai-sang. That's all I can tell, for what good it may do you."

Jen blurted his thanks and ran from the courtyard. Voyaging Moon lived. Nothing else mattered. He would search and find her at all cost.

He halted. To break off his journey now, having come so far? Chai-sang lay in the opposite direction. What if he could not find her? How long would he dare to delay? What of Mafoo and Moxa? Too many questions. He could not gather his wits to think clearly. Then he remembered Master Hu's long lecturing on royal virtues. The old sage would have advised him to press on to T'ien-kuo. To do otherwise—Jen could see Master Hu's frown of disapproval. A prince worthy of his title would not even consider forsaking his duty.

"Yes, that is true," Jen admitted. "Then, as it is true, I am a prince no longer."

He turned south, toward Chai-sang.

◆　◆　◆　◆　◆

An ignoble, unworthy decision. Yet, how can we not forgive a loving heart? Before judging Jen too harshly, continue to the next chapter.

17

*· Jen turns his back on one journey
and his face toward another ·
· Fragrance of Orchid and her grandmother ·*

THERE WAS FIGHTING in the southern districts. As often as local governors ordered out warriors, as often they met with defeat. Some troops deserted, throwing in their lot with a former bandit now arrogantly calling himself the Yellow Scarf King. Peasants whose fields had been trampled, villagers whose dwellings had been ravaged first by one side and then the other, took to the roads and fled northward. They loaded their few possessions into ox carts and barrows, or bore their goods in bundles on their backs.

It was from one of these trains of men and women,

old and young, that Jen heard a name he had forgotten. It came about one evening. Having turned away from T'ien-kuo and set his path for Chai-sang, Jen fell in with a ragged band of folk heading in the opposite direction. Jen himself had been many footsore days on the road when he found them camped for the night in a stubble field, huddled around cook fires. They took him, first, for a straggler from some burned hamlet. When he told them his destination, they took him for a fool.

"Stay clear of Chai-sang," one of the men, a villager, warned. "The Yellow Scarf King's on the march around there."

"No stopping him," put in a rice farmer. "His army gets bigger every day. If he keeps on, he'll be master of the whole country." The farmer shook his head. "You'd think he had a charmed life. I saw him once. He was right in the thick of it, slashing about him with that sword of his. A dozen warriors set on him—he cut them down like grass."

"I heard it told," said the villager, "he rides a dragon instead of a horse. His sword flashes lightning. A magic blade is what they say, big as a tree. Nobody stands against it."

"Dragon? Nonsense." The farmer spat scornfully. "A horse like any other. And he's a man like any other, his real name's Natha. Sword big as a tree? More nonsense. And yet," he added, "there's something strange about that blade. I've seen it slice through a helmet, armor and all. You could almost believe it's magical."

Jen turned away and put down the bowl of food they had given him. For a while, his love of Voyaging Moon had washed away his memory of the cavern. As he squatted by the fire, listening to the farmer talk, it came blazing into his mind.

"It was I," Jen murmured to himself. "I gave him the sword. Because I feared him. Because I feared for my life. I put it in his hands. This is what has come of it."

He tried to reason, telling himself that if he had let Natha kill him the bandit would have taken the sword in any case. Reason did not speak as clearly as shame suddenly did. With that burden, heavier than his bundle of offerings, he set off again the next morning.

"What you can do," one of the men told him, as Jen took his leave, "if you're set on going to Chai-sang, you can try the long way round. Go cross-country to Nang-pei and approach from the east. It's a good bit off your road, but a lot safer."

Jen thought this over. Following that advice would cost him as much as a week. On the other hand, with less risk, he could also manage to find food and shelter in Nang-pei. At last he decided. Weighing possible danger against certain loss of time, he chose to head straight for Chai-sang. He saw no use in turning aside.

And so he did not go to Nang-pei.

During the next couple of days, he grew all the more satisfied that he had chosen well. From others he met on the road, he gathered that Natha and his warriors had fallen back a little, there was a lull in the fighting, and his chances of reaching Chai-sang unhindered were better than before.

This knowledge quickened his steps and brightened his hopes. In Chai-sang, he told himself, he would surely find Voyaging Moon. Together, they would search for Moxa and Mafoo. Even Master Shu might have lived through the storm.

As for T'ien-kuo, he knew he had chosen ignobly. Worse, he did not regret his decision. Someday, he vowed, he would set it right. Reunited with Voyaging Moon, they would cross the Lo and continue their journey. He would not be altogether empty-handed. Three offerings remained. Yuan-ming would grant him an audience. Though Jen had forfeited the right to call himself prince, the words of Master Shu came back to him: Yuan-ming would know him for what he was.

"And yet," he added, "if I am not Jen Shao-yeh, the Young Lord Prince—what am I?"

To this question, he doubted that Master Hu himself could give an answer.

His concerns, in any case, were more immediate: food and a roof. One chilly evening, he stopped at a small farmhouse, having learned that the folk of this district were hospitable to travelers poorer than themselves.

A sturdy, open-faced old woman in cotton skirt and straw sandals greeted him politely. Out of courtesy, she asked nothing of his destination or purposes. Her name, she told him, was Plum Blossom. Jen at first thought she lived here alone. But when his eyes grew accustomed to the dimness of the room, he noticed a low cot. A child was curled on it.

"My granddaughter, Fragrance of Orchid," the woman said as Jen begged pardon for disturbing her sleep. "No, she does not sleep. Nor does she wake. She's lain thus from the day the Yellow Scarves burned our village. Her mother and father were killed. I carried her in my arms to this little property of mine. Here, I thought she would recover. But she neither eats nor drinks, only what I force between her lips. She does not speak, she does not move."

"Is there no way to rouse her?" Jen asked. "Can nothing be done?"

"What have I not done?" replied Plum Blossom. "I've talked to her, sung to her, whispered, pleaded, scolded. I walked miles to find a healer, a herbalist, and brought him here. She is beyond his skill. If she continues unchanged, I am told she will die." Plum Blossom glanced at Jen with fierce determination. "So, I must find some other means."

"Her eyes are open." Jen had stepped quietly to the cot. He bent over the motionless figure, a girl of perhaps ten years. "She sees. She follows the motions of my hand."

"The spirit is lacking," Plum Blossom said. "Without that, can she be called living? Even so, I'll not cease trying to make her live."

"What of toys?" Jen asked. "Her favorite playthings? A doll she loved?"

"Toys? She seldom played with them. Birds were her greatest joy," Plum Blossom said. "She loved to see them fly. She would wave and call to them. Now the birds in these parts are gone, their nests are empty. Fighting and destruction have driven them away."

Jen stood some silent moments watching Fragrance of Orchid. He turned to the old woman. "I have a bird."

Plum Blossom looked at him, puzzled, as Jen undid his bundle. "Not a real bird," he said. "But it can fly."

He took out the kite.

While Plum Blossom, curious, held a lamp for him, he spread the rods and struts on the earthen floor. Working deftly, he put the pieces together. The kite grew to the shape of a bird, its beautifully painted wings wider than Jen's outstretched arms.

He carried the finished kite to Fragrance of Orchid and held it in front of her, moving it back and forth. The girl did not stir. Jen sadly shook his head. He would have turned away, but Plum Blossom snatched his arm.

"Wait! She raises her head."

Indeed, Fragrance of Orchid was struggling to sit up. Her eyes fixed on the kite. She smiled.

Plum Blossom threw her arms around the girl. "Does she live again?"

Jen put down the kite to help the old woman lift the child from her cot. Fragrance of Orchid reached out, murmuring. She bobbed her head happily when Jen brought the plaything to her once more.

All that night, Plum Blossom and Jen stayed at the bedside. Plum Blossom fed the girl, caressed her, and whispered to her. Each time Fragrance of Orchid showed signs of dropping back into her strange sleep, Jen had only to set the kite before her and she would rouse again, all the stronger.

By morning, Fragrance of Orchid was able to stand unaided though unsteady. Beyond a few murmured words, she had not spoken. But her eyes sparkled as Jen led her outside into the farmyard.

There, he flung up the great kite to the freshening breeze. Fragrance of Orchid clapped her hands and laughed with delight to see it soar aloft at the end of its cord. It swooped and swerved, its colors dazzling in the sunlight.

Jen started to haul it back to earth. Fragrance of Orchid shook her head and pointed upward, clearly entreating him to keep it in the air.

"No, I won't fly it anymore," Jen said quietly to her. "You'll do it." He took her hand and curled her fingers around the cord. "Keep this. It is yours."

* * * * *

A gift meant for Yuan-ming has found its way into the hands of a child. But who could wish Jen to have done otherwise? To learn more about the kite and Fragrance of Orchid, leave Jen for the time being and read the next chapter.

18

• *The Tale of the Soaring Kite* •

THE MOMENT FRAGRANCE OF ORCHID felt the tug of the kite as it flew aloft, her strength began returning. Her eyes brightened, and she laughed to see it dip and veer in the breeze.

"My tame bird!" cried Fragrance of Orchid. "See, it will do whatever I ask."

"You are a little bird yourself," replied Grandmother Plum Blossom, beaming to see the girl happy and high-spirited again. "A marvelous gift! What a shame the young man left so quickly. We had no time to thank him enough. Even so, we must always remember him."

"I will," Fragrance of Orchid said. She could, in fact, recall his every feature, for the stranger's face was one of the first things she saw after the kite roused her. "But why did he have a kite with him in the first place?"

"Who can tell?" replied Plum Blossom. "We can only be glad he did. Come now, bring down your new plaything before you tire yourself."

Fragrance of Orchid obeyed, although reluctantly. No sooner did the kite touch ground than her face clouded and her eyes lost their sparkle. Plum Blossom could see her granddaughter's heart grow heavy when, moments before, it had been so light.

That evening, while she did not fall back into her trancelike sleep, Fragrance of Orchid sat motionless and silent, gazing wistfully at the kite.

"If the toy so cheers her," Plum Blossom thought, "then let her play with it as often as she likes."

Next morning, therefore, Plum Blossom did not burden the girl with household tasks, but allowed her to fly the kite to her heart's content.

Each day thereafter, Fragrance of Orchid sprang out of bed at the crack of dawn, ran outdoors, and flung the kite into the breeze. And, each day, her strength and spirits grew better.

Also, the more she played with the kite the more skill she gained in flying it. The slightest movement of her fingers on the string made the bright wings dip and dance, pitch and plunge as if alive.

"Almost a real bird!" Fragrance of Orchid cried. "It flies of itself!"

So, indeed, it seemed. At first, to let it catch the wind, Fragrance of Orchid raced across the farmyard and outlying fields, paying out the line as she sped lightly over the ground. But soon she realized that she need only toss it a little above her head, and the kite would soar immediately skyward.

One day, Fragrance of Orchid went as usual into the fields. Before she could raise the kite, suddenly it leaped from her hands and went circling upward.

The string whipped through her fingers so rapidly it burned them. Fragrance of Orchid nevertheless did not let go. She bent all her strength to hold on to the taut line. She tugged and strained, doing her best to haul the kite earthward, but it climbed ever higher. Though she dug her heels into the ground, the kite soon pulled her along on her tiptoes, sweeping her across the dry grass.

Within moments, the kite flew so high that it went to the full length of its string. Fragrance of Orchid, however, clung to the end of the line. Otherwise, she would have to let the kite fly away; and this she was determined not to do.

"Sail high as you like," Fragrance of Orchid cried. "If you won't come down, I'll come up after you."

Fragrance of Orchid tried to climb up the kite

string. Even as she did, she felt herself lifted from the earth. Her toes no longer touched the ground. Still clutching the string, she skimmed over the field. The kite bore her higher and higher, above the tallest trees in the fringe of woodland.

Hearing her granddaughter's voice, Plum Blossom ran from the farmhouse. In a quick downward glance, Fragrance of Orchid saw the old woman wave her arms, then set off to follow as fast as her legs could carry her.

"Grandmother Plum Blossom will find me once I come down," Fragrance of Orchid told herself. And so she clung bravely to the string even as the kite rose far above hills and forests. Those first moments, as the ground fell away beneath her, she shut her eyes tightly, not daring to look down. As the kite sped along, she ventured to open them again. She found herself above a shoreless ocean of clouds under a bright blue sky stretching farther than she could see. Sunlight poured over her, the wind sang songs in her ears. Instead of being frightened, she laughed with joy as she soared higher than birds had ever flown.

How long, how far the kite carried her, Fragrance of Orchid could not guess. But now the kite began dipping slowly downward. She passed through towers and castles of clouds and saw, just below, the high peaks of mountains. The kite dropped toward the rocky face of the tallest, and the girl braced herself, expecting to be dashed against the crags. The kite, however, lowered her gently into a huge nest of branches, twigs, and leaves.

The line slackened without her weight on it, and the kite glided down to land beside her.

"So," Fragrance of Orchid said, "you've decided to come back, have you? Very well, you flew me here and you can fly me out again."

She held the kite up, as she had often done before. It did not rise again.

"Then," said Fragrance of Orchid, "I'll have to find my own way down."

First, she thought of tying the kite string around one of the jagged rocks and lowering herself on it. She quickly calculated the string was too short to reach anywhere near the ground. Before she could devise some other means, she glimpsed a bird flying rapidly toward her.

As it drew closer, she saw it was an enormous eagle. Its feathers glittered like burnished gold, its eyes flashed like diamonds, and its outspread wings beat so powerfully that wind whistled through the crags.

Fragrance of Orchid forgot her own predicament to marvel at the sight. Never had she seen so magnificent a bird; nor was she frightened in the least when the eagle sped to the nest and landed at her side.

Folding its wings, the eagle turned its eyes on Fragrance of Orchid, who gazed back in fascination.

"What is this?" the eagle said. "A new chick in my nest?"

Fragrance of Orchid was hardly surprised to hear the eagle speak, for she had always believed that birds could talk. So it seemed only natural, and no stranger than being carried away by a kite.

"I am Niang-niang, she-eagle of Mount Wu-shan," the great bird continued. "And you are the fledgling Fragrance of Orchid."

This surprised the girl more than anything else. "Yes, I am," she said, "but how is it that you know my name?"

"I know many things," replied Niang-niang. "I have observed you often during my flights here and there. What I have not seen for myself, my fellow creatures of the air have told me. I know, for example, you shared your food with the winter birds when they found nothing to eat. I also know that once, in the bird market, you opened the cages. Oh, yes, and were punished for it, too."

Fragrance of Orchid nodded, for all this was true. "Niang-niang," she replied courteously, "as you know so much, do you know one thing more? How shall I climb down from here and find my way home?"

Niang-niang shook her golden head. "Little fledgling, I may not tell you. Nor am I certain you shall do so. Had you let go the kite string and let it fly free instead of clutching it, things would have gone otherwise. Now they are what they are and what they must be."

Fragrance of Orchid had so far kept courage in the face of all that had happened. Hearing these words, however, she felt her heart must break, as now she feared she had lost kindred and home past recovery.

"What is lost may, with hope, be found again," said Niang-niang, as if reading her thoughts. "Were I permitted, I would carry you where you wish. That is forbidden to me. I cannot change the path you follow, though it may or may not lead you back to earth.

"Stay with me," the eagle urged. "The sky is vaster than the earth, as you will see. You, who have so loved and befriended all birds, would you not care to be one of us?"

"How is that possible?" Fragrance of Orchid said. "Even if I wanted, I can't fly."

"You can," said Niang-niang. The eagle then instructed the girl to untie the kite string and take firm hold of the wooden rods and struts that made the frame of the silken wings.

"Now what shall I do?" asked Fragrance of Orchid, having followed Niang-niang's directions.

"Very simple," Niang-niang said. "Climb from the nest. Dive into the air as if into a pool of water."

Fragrance of Orchid hesitated. A glance at the ground so far below made her head spin.

"Do as every fledgling must," Niang-niang said. "If you trust what I tell you, no harm will come to you."

Fragrance of Orchid was fearful despite the eagle's reassurance. Nevertheless, plucking up her courage, she climbed over the rim of the nest, took a deep breath, and resolutely sprang into empty air.

At first, she plummeted downward, gripping the spinning kite as she sped past the crags to the forest floor. Within moments, however, she felt the kite lift and begin to soar into the clouds. Her fear vanished and she laughed with joy as she swooped and circled, sailing on the air tides with Niang-niang flying beside.

"Enough now, little fledgling," the eagle called. "You have begun well. There is much more to learn."

Fragrance of Orchid reluctantly followed the eagle back to the nest, sorry to leave the air and eager to fly again. Niang-niang promised they would venture farther next time. And so Fragrance of Orchid curled up in the nest and slept that night under the soft warmth of the eagle's wing.

Each day thereafter, Niang-niang brought the girl food and cared for her as if Fragrance of Orchid were an eaglet. And, each day, they flew still greater distances. Sometimes they joined flocks of sparrows, swallows, or ravens, who dipped their wings in recognition and called out fondly to the girl, delighted to see her among them in the sky.

"You fly well," Niang-niang said. "Now you must learn to see, farther and clearer than you have ever done before."

"Gladly," said Fragrance of Orchid, "but how shall I do so?"

"Again, very simple," Niang-niang said. "To begin to see, you must first begin to look."

Fragrance of Orchid puzzled over what Niang-niang told her. Nevertheless, during their flights, she tried her best to look carefully at the fields, hills, and woodlands that spread beneath her. Little by little, her vision sharpened. One day, as they swooped through a bank of clouds, Fragrance of Orchid cried out in amazement:

"I see fish swimming in the river! And there, a woman feeding chickens in a farmyard. And there, a town," she called, as they flew onward. "The houses, the streets. I see children racing. Ah, one of them tripped and skinned her knees! And there, a fruit seller giving change to a customer. I can count the coins in his hand." Fragrance of Orchid laughed. "It's not the right change, either. There's the buyer arguing. Now they've settled it."

"Your eyes have grown almost as sharp as mine," said Niang-niang. "Having learned to see, now you must learn to understand."

Girl and eagle continued their flights, farther and farther, sometimes resting on a mountain peak, sometimes flying all night long under moon and stars.

"Are we still in the Kingdom of T'ang?" Fragrance of Orchid said. "Have we left it and crossed into some other kingdom?"

"The first thing to understand," Niang-niang said, "is that there is no Kingdom of T'ang, nor any other realm. Do you see borders? Is one countryside so different from another? Is not a mountain a mountain, a tree a tree, wherever it may be? Kingdoms? They are pitiful inventions of humankind. They mean nothing to us. We see there is only the world itself, nothing more, nothing less."

Fragrance of Orchid saw this, too, with her own eyes. Also, she saw much more. She saw the earth turn, from sunrise to sunset. She saw many mountains, and learned they sprang from the same root. She saw many rivers, and learned they were only arms of the same river; and that the greatest oceans merged with all other oceans.

And so, Fragrance of Orchid, with the great eagle always at her side, lived her days aloft, sleeping in tree-tops or mountain peaks, setting foot on ground only to find food and drink.

Each new sight and each new discovery delighted her. Happy though she was, her thoughts turned ever homeward. She wondered if, during her flights, she might someday catch sight of Grandmother Plum Blossom, and if they would be together again.

"Even my keen eyes cannot see so far ahead," Niang-niang replied.

Nevertheless, Fragrance of Orchid stayed watchful for any sign of Grandmother Plum Blossom.

"If I look hard enough, and see clearly enough," said Fragrance of Orchid, "sooner or later I must find her."

"If that is where your path leads you in the end," replied Niang-niang, "then you surely will."

♦ ♦ ♦ ♦ ♦

Leaving Fragrance of Orchid high in the air, we now return to the ground, where we left Jen on his way to Chai-sang. Whether he reaches there or not, and what happens to him in the meanwhile, is told in the following chapter.

19

· Jen holds an umbrella ·
· Chen-cho paints a picture ·
· An invitation to dinner ·

FOR SOME DAYS AFTER LEAVING Grandmother Plum
Blossom and Fragrance of Orchid, Jen pressed on toward Chai-sang. Sometimes he slept in the encamp-
ments of fleeing peasants and villagers, but as often as
not, he bedded down in the underbrush amid the fallen
leaves of autumn. Someone had given him a length of
quilt. Nights, he rolled up in it; days, he wrapped it
around his shoulders and belted it with a rope at his
waist. A raw north wind had risen, nipping at him as
he struck cross-country over fields crackling with
morning frost under heavy purple clouds.

The first snow showers began as he made his way through a narrow valley, past low brown hills and bare trees. Until now, after leaving the roads, he had come upon no other travelers. But here, beside a shallow stream, he stopped short. For all his discomfort, he could not help laughing.

A young man in quilted jacket and felt cap with earflaps jutting like wings squatted on the turf. With one hand, he tried to keep a sheaf of papers from blowing away; with the other, he attempted to put up an umbrella. He was not succeeding at either task.

"Don't stand there gawking and grinning, fool! Lend a hand," the stranger called, just before the umbrella collapsed over his head and he disappeared into the folds.

Jen hurried toward him, helping to keep the papers from flying off and to disentangle its owner from the octopus clutches of the umbrella.

"Excellent. That should do it." Having crawled out, the youth securely raised his portable canopy and settled his cap on his head. "Untrustworthy contraption. It attacks me out of sheer malice. When I paint, I use it to keep the sun out of my eyes, you understand."

"I'd understand better," Jen said, laughing, "if the sun were shining. It pleased you to call me a fool, but I wonder which of us is the greater."

"I meant it only in a friendly sense. Since there are more fools than wise men, I assumed it more likely you were one of the former. But, you're right. No sun, of

course not. I should have said snow. Let us now scruti-
nize and determine if my latest effort is completely
ruined."

Chen-cho, as he named himself, took up the scroll
he had been working on. Jen saw the beginnings of a
landscape painting, done with a few bold strokes and,
here and there, splashes of muted earth colors. Unfin-
ished, Jen recognized it was nonetheless beautifully
done and complimented the artist on his work.

"You like it? Tell me, then, what shall it be called?"
Chen-cho was about Jen's age and stature, with a good-
natured face and quick, wry smile. The deep lines at the
corners of his eyes may have resulted from squinting far
into the distance or peering closely at his handiwork.
"Ten Thousand Blotches? The snow drops have melted
all over it. But—no, not ruined at all. Better than I
could have done on purpose. Now, if your honorable
self would favor me by holding this accursed umbrella
over my head—"

Jen did as Chen-cho asked. The artist worked
quickly, making the wet spots and stains a part of the
picture. Jen shook his head in admiration. Chen-cho
merely shrugged, declaring that someday he would do a
better one. With that, he packed up his materials, bal-
anced the umbrella on his shoulder like a spear, and invited Jen to come with him to the nearby village of
Ping-erh.

"You look as if you could stand a good meal,"
Chen-cho said as they walked along. "I'm staying at a

reasonably acceptable inn. That is, the food won't poison you. The landlord will put you up for the night, if you want. He still owes me for the work I did for him."

From this, Jen assumed that Chen-cho had bargained one of his pictures for food and lodging. The artist chuckled when Jen asked him if such was the case.

"No, no, better than that," Chen-cho replied. "I painted his door. Not a picture of it. I mean that I painted it with red lacquer. Also, I wrote out a piece of calligraphy for him, a magical charm: 'Protect this dwelling from dragons.' The fellow's quite happy with it, he's convinced it works. In fact, it does," Chen-cho added, with a wink. "There's not a single dragon anywhere in the neighborhood.

"And you, Honorable Ragbag—your name's Jen, you said?" the painter went on. "What's your occupation? A prosperous merchant in disguise? No. A government official? Hardly. You look seedy enough to be an honest fellow."

Jen laughed. "I have no occupation. No longer. I'm searching for someone. A flute girl. And my friends."

"Search away, good luck to you," Chen-cho said. "I also search. In my case, for landscapes to paint. This one's interesting. Bleak, at first; but, if you look at it the right way, quite marvelous. Someday, I'd like to do the Lotus Bridge in Ch'ang-an, or the Happy Phoenix Gardens near the river. I've heard they're very fine."

"Yes, so they are." Jen's heart turned suddenly heavy at the recollection. "I'd almost forgotten."

"You've been there?" Chen-cho said, impressed. "You've seen them? You'll tell me more of them later. A merry dinner will jog your memory."

Chen-cho rambled on, gossiping, telling tales and jokes. His contagious high spirits lifted Jen's own. The two travelers had become good companions by the time they reached Ping-erh.

At the inn, however, they found no merry dinner, nor cheer of any kind. Villagers filled the little square, scurrying in all directions. Some had grimly begun loading household goods into carts and barrows.

"Closed! Closed!" The landlord waved his arms as Jen and Chen-cho stepped into the eating room. "Out! Be off while you can!"

◆ ◆ ◆ ◆ ◆

Jen has struck up a pleasant friendship with the good-natured Chen-cho, but it seems both will have to go without their dinner. Why such alarm? To find out, read the next chapter.

20

· Pebble and avalanche ·
· Meeting with an old enemy ·
· Parting from a new friend ·

"BE OFF?" CRIED CHEN-CHO. "Off nowhere till we have our dinner."

The landlord paid no further attention and went back to tearing his hair and yelling at his servants to pack up all they could carry. Some local men and women had come into the eating room, where they stood talking urgently among themselves. While Chen-cho still protested at missing his dinner, Jen hurried to ask them the cause of such alarm.

"Where have you been all day? Living on the

moon?" retorted a big-framed peasant whose name, Jen learned, was Chang. "My elder brother brought me word this morning. The Yellow Scarf King's riding with his advance guard, so the rest of his army isn't far behind. I'd reckon he'll be here in two day's time at most."

Jen questioned Chang more closely, gathering from his account that Natha meant to take Ping-erh for a winter headquarters.

"I say let him have it," put in one of the villagers. "Our officials didn't waste time scuttling off, so neither will I. That Yellow Scarf devil won't find me here."

"I'm sure he won't, you turtle," one of the peasant women flung at him. "Turn tail, the lot of you. Don't stand up to him. No, don't give that a thought."

"Here, now, he doesn't speak for all of us," Chang said. "I'd stand up to him, if any stand with me."

"Against a natural man, I would," said a farmer. "He's no human being, he's all devil. That's what I've heard. And that sword of his! He got it from the king of devils himself."

"He's a man, no more nor less than you are," Jen broke in. He turned to Chang. "Any to stand with you? I will."

"Hear that?" exclaimed the woman. "This fellow's a stranger, but he puts our own men to shame."

"You're only one," Chang said to Jen. "That's—"

"That's two, counting you," Jen said.

"That's three," put in the woman, "counting me."

"There's enough of you, Mourning Dove, to make three by yourself," a villager called out to her. "Best go back and tend your chickens. What do you know about any of this?"

"I know enough to guard the henhouse door when the fox is on the prowl," said Mourning Dove.

At this, a handful of locals began disputing among themselves. Chen-cho, giving up all hope of a meal, had been eavesdropping on the conversation. He drew Jen aside.

"What are you up to?" he muttered. "You're not a fool, you're an idiot. Natha Yellow Scarf? You don't know who you're dealing with."

"I know," Jen said. "I bought my life from him. I think I might have paid too high a price."

Leaving the artist to puzzle over that, Jen went to the villagers. Mourning Dove and Chang had already persuaded most of those present to stand against Natha.

"The others?" Jen asked. "Will they stay, too?"

"If they believe there's a chance of holding him off," Mourning Dove said.

"It also works the other way round," Jen said. "There's no chance of holding him off if they don't stay. Go into the square. Tell them there's a way they might save the village."

"Is there?" asked Chang.

"There could be," Jen said, "if enough of them help."

"I'll see they do," Mourning Dove declared. She

strode out to the square, Chang and Jen following. They pressed through the crowd. Mourning Dove climbed atop an ox cart and tried to make herself heard above the commotion. At first, the villagers paid little heed, but as the peasant woman's voice rose, more and more paused to listen. Chen-cho had come out to observe, and the painter shook his head in surprised admiration.

"You're the one who put her up to this, but she's doing well on her own." The artist chuckled. "Had I any taste for this kind of thing—which, luckily, I don't—I'd be tempted to lend her a hand."

"You will," Jen said. "I have a thought, and I need you and your brush to put it on paper."

Jen led the painter to the inn. Mourning Dove, Chang, and half a dozen others, who had formed a makeshift council of war, soon hurried back with news: Most of the villagers had chosen to stay. By this time, following Jen's instructions, Chen-cho had sketched out in workable details what had been only vague ideas in Jen's mind.

"I had an old teacher once," Jen said, as the artist tucked his box of brushes and pigments back into his jacket. "He taught me the history of T'ang. I was a slow student, but I remember his tale of the warriors long ago who defended Ch'ang-an against invaders when the city was no more than a village like this. It could help us now. We'll need carpenters, woodcutters, rope-makers."

"You'll have them," said Mourning Dove, examining the sketches and nodding approval. She sent Chang to rally as many artisans as he could find, then turned her attention to matters Jen had not considered.

He listened to her, astonished. Mourning Dove, as she frankly admitted, could neither read nor write. At first glance, she would have been taken as no more than a farm wife who only knew to count eggs. But she had already calculated the strength of the villagers and planned out their positioning, how best they should be divided, and how the outlying forests and streams could be used to their advantage. She had guessed at the number of Natha's advance guard and the path they would most likely follow.

"I know a general," Jen remarked to Chen-cho. "The best of warriors. I doubt that he'd have done better."

"First, you say you know the Yellow Scarf King," replied Chen-cho. "Now, a general. Honorable Ragbag, allow me to ask: Who the devil are you?"

"If I knew for certain," Jen said, "I'd tell you."

Jen sat astride the horse he had asked for. Mourning Dove had given him the best in the village. In the first raw light of dawn, he huddled the quilt around his shoulders. He had asked for a weapon as well, and Chang had found a blade from the abandoned yamen. It would serve. He had put Yuan-ming's sword in Natha's hands. He would have it back again.

The horse whickered and blew white smoke from its nostrils. Chen-cho and a party of villagers stamped their feet and beat their arms against the chill. All day and all night, the artisans of Ping-erh had worked to build wooden frameworks bristling with long, sharpened poles wrapped in oil-soaked straw. Dozens of such barriers had been hidden along the forest fringe, at every pathway leading toward the village. At other gaps, the folk of Ping-erh had hewed down trees, piling trunks and branches into dense barricades.

Mourning Dove, in a heavy jacket, a cloth knotted around her head, had given a last sharp scrutiny to the frames. She stood, hands on hips, beside Jen.

"We've done all as you showed us, young scholar," Mourning Dove said, having decided for herself that such was Jen's occupation. "I'm not rash enough to think we can battle Yellow Scarf's warriors hand to hand."

"No, but you can turn them away," Jen said. "Make Natha see Ping-erh's too much trouble, not worth his effort."

"Oh, we'll show him how troublesome we can be." Mourning Dove grinned, pushed up her sleeves, and went to talk quietly with each one of the grim-faced, restless villagers. Jen strained his ears for the sound of horsemen. A pebble may stop an avalanche, Master Hu once told him. The folk of Ping-erh were small pebbles, but here the avalanche must either halt or crush them. This portion of the forest was the last easy access to the village. Beyond, a line of rugged hills barred the way.

Jen stiffened in the saddle. The notes of a bugle pierced the air. That would be from Chang, at the opposite end of the woodland, where Mourning Dove had expected Natha's first approach. Moments later, Jen heard distant shouting. Black trails of smoke rose above the treetops. Chang and his people had set their barrier ablaze. If the plan worked, each party of villagers, one after the other, would set their own frameworks alight. Each entry would be barred by a wall of fire whenever Natha and his warriors sought to turn and make their way through some other woodland path. They would find gate after flaming gate flung shut against them.

Mourning Dove raised her arm. By now, Jen heard hoofbeats. The warriors would be galloping along the fringe of woods. Now, at Mourning Dove's signal, the villagers brought torches to their barricades. The wrappings, soaked with oil and pitch, burst into flames. Natha and his men were clearly in sight. Jen saw the leading horsemen rein up their mounts. The animals reared, heads tossing, eyes rolling in terror of the fire. The riders kicked vainly at their steeds' flanks; the horses shied away. He glimpsed Natha, his face scowling under his gleaming helmet of lacquered leather. He halted an instant, glaring at the barrier. Then he spat scornfully and signaled his warriors to fall back.

The villagers roared in triumph. Mourning Dove, calling out joyfully, ran toward Jen. He did not wait.

Another moment and Natha would be amid his retreating warriors. Jen galloped from the fringe of trees.

"Natha! Natha Yellow Scarf!"

Natha wheeled and pulled up his mount, staring curiously at the lone horseman bearing down on him. He grinned with amusement, as if observing the progress of some audacious bug, but gave not the faintest sign of recognition as Jen galloped closer.

Gripping his blade, Jen pressed on. With a movement almost leisurely, Natha drew his sword. Jen plunged headlong, only at the last moment wheeling his horse broadside of Natha as he swung the blade with all his might.

Natha's sword flashed quicker than Jen's eyes could follow. There was a grating clash of blade on blade. Jen cried out as the shock numbed his arm. His weapon had been cut in two. He stared at the useless hilt in his hand. Natha raised his sword again.

Jen heard hoofbeats behind him and someone shouting at the top of his voice. A rider drew up beside him: Chen-cho.

"Get back, Ragbag!" The painter snatched at Jen's bridle.

Natha, surprised for an instant, hesitated, then swung up the sword again. Chen-cho's hand darted into his jacket. He snatched out his paint box and flung it straight at Natha's face. The Yellow Scarf King's head jerked back, his sword stroke wavered the fraction of a moment; then he slashed at this makeshift missile, his blade moving so swiftly the wooden container scattered in a blur of splinters.

Chen-cho had by then kicked his own horse and Jen's into a gallop, and they sped for the safety of the woodlands. Without so much as a backward glance at this pair of annoying gnats, Natha turned his steed and cantered to rejoin his departing warriors.

"Ragbag, you are a true simpleton," Chen-cho remarked as they gained the skirt of trees. "I take it you had a score to settle. It must have been a large one, but you're an idiot if you thought you'd take him on by yourself."

"I did, once," Jen said. "And failed. Now, failed again." He flung away the shattered sword. "No matter, I should thank you for saving my life, whatever that may be worth."

"There's enthusiastic gratitude," Chen-cho said. "All right, then: You're welcome."

They rode back to Ping-erh with Mourning Dove and the villagers rejoicing that Natha had turned away to seek a less troublesome target. Jen paid little heed to the festive crowd in the square. He retrieved his bundle while Chen-cho gathered up his papers and umbrella. When he asked where the painter would go next, Chen-cho shrugged.

"I'd have stayed here a while," said the artist. "There were a few more scenes I wanted to do. Your Yellow Scarf friend has more or less put me out of my occupation. That sword of his turned my brushes into matchwood. But, I'll find others."

"You already have." Jen undid the bundle, which had grown small and light by now. Unhesitating, though with a half smile of sadness, he put the sandal-wood box into the painter's hands.

"Here, what's this?" Chen-cho exclaimed. "What's a fellow like you doing with such a thing? Are you also a painter and never let on?"

Jen shook his head. "I had it for another purpose. I think you can make better use of it."

Chen-cho had opened the box to examine the brush, ink stick, and ink stone. "Honorable Ragbag, I can tell you're no artist, or you'd never have parted with this. Wonderful! Look here, have you the least idea what these are?"

By then, Jen had waved a farewell and was gone from the inn, setting off on his way again.

＊　＊　＊　＊　＊

Leaving our hero to continue his search, with one gift fewer than before, we turn our attention to Chen-cho and the sandalwood box. What has the artist seen that so pleases him? To find out, read the next chapter.

21

· *The Tale of the Tiger's Paintbrush* ·

CHEN-CHO THE PAINTER was a good-natured, easy-going sort. He liked his food and drink, though as often as not he did without either. Not because he suffered any lack of customers. He was, in fact, a most excellent artist, and many who saw his pictures wished eagerly to buy them. To Chen-cho, however, parting with one of his landscapes was like having a tooth pulled. Sometimes, of course, he was obliged to do so, when he needed a few strings of cash to keep body and soul together—although usually he spent the money on paper and paint. On the other hand, out of sudden impulse or foolish whim, he was just as likely to give away one of his pictures to a passerby who wistfully admired but could ill afford to purchase it.

For the rest, he was a little absentminded, his head so filled with colors and shapes that he lost track of time, forgot to wash his face or change his clothes. With his collapsing umbrella, his felt cap, his bespattered trousers flapping around his ankles, he became a familiar sight in towns and villages where he stopped in the course of his wanderings. Children tagged after him, fascinated to peer over his shoulder as he worked. Local officials, however, felt more comfortable after he left.

Now, with the sandalwood box on the table in front of him, paying no attention to the rejoicing villagers crowding the inn, Chen-cho gleefully scrutinized his gift. As an artist, he had immediately recognized the excellence of the materials, but he studied them again to confirm his first opinion.

He picked up the stick of black ink and rolled it around in his fingers. He sniffed at it, even tasted it, and licked his lips as if it were some delicious morsel.

"Marvelous!" Chen-cho said to himself. "Perfect! No question, this ink's made from the ashes of pine trees on the south slope of Mount Lu, the very best."

Next, he turned his attention to the ink stone, with its shallow little basin for water at one end and its flat surface for grinding the solid ink at the other. The stone was fine-grained, flawless; and, in color, an unusual reddish gray. Chen-cho rubbed his thumb over it lovingly and shook his head in amazement.

"Here's a treasure in itself! I've heard of stones like this. They come only from one place: a grotto in Mount Wu-shan. I never believed they were more than legend. Yet, I have one right in my hand."

Chuckling over his good fortune, blessing the stranger he had fondly nicknamed Honorable Ragbag, the painter picked up the last object in the box: a paintbrush with a long bamboo handle.

"This is odd." Chen-cho squinted at the brush hairs, tested them on the palm of his hand and the tip of his nose. "Soft? Firm? Both at once? What's it made of? Not rabbit fur, not wolf hair, not mouse whiskers."

The painter could not restrain himself another moment. He called the landlord for a cup of water, poured a little into the basin of the ink stone, then carefully rubbed the tip of the ink stick against the grinding surface. No matter how much he rubbed, the stick showed no trace of wear.

"At this rate," he said to himself, "it will last forever. One stick, and ink enough for the rest of my life. There's frugality for you!"

He pulled out a sheet of paper. Moistening the brush, rolling the tip in the ink he had ground, he made a couple of trial strokes. As he did, a thrill began at the tip of his toes, raced to his arm, his hand, his fingers. The sensation turned him giddy. He glanced at the paper. His jaw dropped. The brush strokes were not black. They were bright vermilion.

"I'd have sworn that ink was black," Chen-cho murmured. "Was I mistaken? Yes, no doubt. The light's dim here."

He made a few more brush strokes. They were no longer vermilion, but jade green. Chen-cho put down the brush and rubbed his chin.

"What's happening here? That ink stick's black as night, through and through. What's doing it? The stone? The brush? No matter, let's have another go."

Chen-cho daubed at the paper, which was soon covered with streaks of bright orange, red, and blue. Anyone else might have grown alarmed or frightened at such an uncanny happening. But Chen-cho enjoyed surprises, mysteries, and extraordinary events. And so he laughed with delight to find himself owner of these remarkable materials.

"Well, old fellow," he said to himself, "you've come onto something you never expected and probably better than you deserve. Let's try something else. Those are marvelous colors, but what if I wanted a sort of lilac purple-green with a reddish cast?"

No sooner did Chen-cho imagine such a hue than it flowed from his brush. He quickly discovered that he need only envision whatever shade he wanted, and there it was, from brush to paper.

"That's what I call convenient and efficient," exclaimed the joyous Chen-cho. "No more paint pots and a dozen different pigments. Here's everything all at once."

With that, he clapped his felt hat firmly on his head, seized a handful of papers, packed up the box, and hurried out of the inn. He ran all the way to the stream where he had first met Ragbag. There he settled himself, ignoring the weather, forgetting to put up his umbrella, and worked away happily, letting the brush go as it wished, hardly glancing at what he was doing.

It was dusk and the light had faded before he could make himself leave off. But the picture was finished, better than anything he had ever painted. Chen-cho laughed and slapped his leg. "Old boy," he told himself, "keep on like this and you might even do something worthwhile."

He went back to his room at the inn. Excited by his wonderful new possessions, he forgot to eat his dinner. He barely slept that night, eager to start another picture.

Next morning and for several days thereafter, Chen-cho went into the countryside looking for scenes to paint. Each landscape that took shape under his hand delighted him more than the one before.

It snowed heavily on a certain morning. Chen-cho usually paid no mind to bad weather. That day, the wind blew so sharply and the snow piled up so deeply that he decided to stay in his room. Nevertheless, his fingers itched to take up the brush. Ordinarily, he painted outdoors, according to whatever vista caught his eye. This time, he thought to do something else.

"Why not make up my own landscape? I'll paint whatever pops into my head and strikes my fancy."

Taking one of his largest sheets of paper, he set about painting hills and valleys, forests and streams, adding glens and lakes wherever it pleased him. He painted rolling meadows he had never seen; and bright banks of flowers he invented as he went along; and clouds of fantastic shapes, all drenched in sunlight, with a couple of rainbows added for good measure.

"What this may be, I've no idea," Chen-cho said when he finished. He blinked happily at the picture. "All I know is: I've astonished myself. That's something that never happened before."

Chen-cho could not take his eyes from his handiwork. He peered at it from every angle, first from a distance, then so close he bumped his nose.

"If I didn't know better," he said, "I'd swear I could smell those flowers. In fact, if I hadn't painted them, I'd believe I could pick one."

He reached out, pretending to pluck a blossom. Next thing he knew, the flower lay in his hand.

Chen-cho gaped at it. He swallowed hard, then grinned and shook his head. "What you've done, you foolish fellow, is go to sleep on your feet. You're having a dream. A marvelous one, but that's all it is."

He pinched himself, rubbed his eyes, soaked his head in a basin of water, paced back and forth. The flower was still where he had set it on the table. Fragrance filled the room.

"I'm wide-awake, no question about it," he finally

admitted. He went again to the picture. "That being the case, let's examine this reasonably. It seems I've put my hand into it. What, for example, if I did—this?"

Chen-cho poked his head into the painted landscape. Indeed, he could look around him at the trees and lakes. The sunshine dazzled and warmed him. He sniffed the fragrant air. He heard the rush of a waterfall somewhere in the distance.

"This is definitely out of the ordinary," Chen-cho murmured, pulling back his head. "Dare I explore a little farther?"

With that, Chen-cho plucked up his courage and stepped all the way into the picture.

He was not certain how he did it. The painting was large, but far from as large as the artist himself. Yet, it must have grown spacious enough to take him in, for there he was, standing knee-deep in the soft grass of a meadow.

"So far so good," he said. "But now I've gone in—how do I get out?"

He answered his own question by easily stepping back into the room. His first apprehension gave way to delight as he discovered that he could walk in and out of the painting as often as he pleased.

With each venture into the landscape, Chen-cho found himself becoming all the more comfortable and confident.

"It's quite amazing, hard to believe," Chen-cho remarked. "But I suppose one can get used to anything, including miracles."

A fascinating thought sprang to mind. What, he wondered, lay beyond the fields and forests and across the valleys?

"I've no idea what's there," he said, "which is the best reason to go and find out."

Chen-cho picked up the sandalwood box and a sheaf of paper in case he found some especially attractive scene. Stepping into the landscape, he set off eagerly along a gentle path that opened at his feet. He soon came to a high-arched bridge over a stream lined with willows. The view so charmed him that he spread his paper and began to paint.

He stopped in the middle of a brush stroke. He had the impression of being watched. When he turned around, he saw that his impression was correct.

Sitting on its haunches, observing him through a pair of orange eyes, was an enormous tiger.

"Hello there, Chen-cho." The tiger padded toward him, stripes rippling at every fluid pace. "My name is Lao-hu. I've been expecting you."

"A pleasure to make your acquaintance," replied Chen-cho. Having by now grown accustomed to marvelous happenings, the arrival of a tiger did not unsettle him too much, especially since the big animal had addressed him in a friendly tone. "However, I can't truthfully say I was expecting you."

"You must have, whether you knew it or not," Lao-hu said. "Otherwise, I wouldn't be here. Ah. I see you've been using my brush."

"Yours?"

"My hairs," Lao-hu said. "From the tip of my tail. I hope it pleases you."

"A remarkable brush," Chen-cho said. "I'd go so far as to call it miraculous. From the tip of your tail? Yes, but in that case, I'm a little puzzled. I hope you don't mind my asking, but if you weren't here until I painted this picture, where were you before I painted it? If you were someplace else, how did you get here? And who plucked out those hairs in the first place?"

"Why concern yourself with details?" Lao-hu yawned enormously. "It's a tedious, boring matter you wouldn't understand to begin with. Let me just say this: You're not the first to paint such a picture, nor the last. Many have done still finer work. And you're certainly not the first to use my brush."

"Tell me, then," Chen-cho said, "can others find their way into my picture? A question of privacy, you understand."

"Of course they can," replied Lao-hu. "It's your painting, but now that you've done it, it's open to anybody who cares to enter. But leave that idle speculation and nit-picking to scholars who enjoy such occupation. You've hardly seen the smallest part of all this"—Lao-hu motioned around him with his long tail—"so let me show you a little, for a start. Climb on my back."

Chen-cho gladly accepted the tiger's invitation. Lao-hu sprang across the stream in one mighty leap. Chen-cho clamped his legs around the tiger's flanks and his arms around Lao-hu's powerful neck. The tiger sped across meadows, through forests, up and down hills. Chen-cho glimpsed garden pavilions, farmhouses, towns and villages, sailboats on rivers, birds in the air, fish leaping in brooks, animals of every kind. Some of what he saw looked vaguely familiar; the rest, altogether strange and fascinating. Lao-hu promised they would continue their explorations and carried the painter back to where they had started.

As easily as he had stepped into the painting, Chen-cho stepped into the room. Lao-hu followed, much to the surprise and delight of the painter, who was reluctant to part from his new companion.

"I can go wherever I please," Lao-hu replied when Chen-cho asked about this, "just as you can."

"Can other people see you?" asked Chen-cho, wondering what his landlord might say if he came into the room and found a tiger.

"Of course they can," Lao-hu said. "I may be a magical tiger, but I'm not an invisible one."

With that, Lao-hu curled up at the foot of Chen-cho's bed. The tired but happy painter flung himself down and went to sleep, thinking that, all in all, it had been an interesting day.

Next morning, when the storm had passed, Chen-cho packed his belongings and set off on his way again. Lao-hu had jumped back into the picture, which the artist had rolled up and carried under his arm. Once away from the village, Chen-cho unrolled the painting. He saw no sign of Lao-hu. Dismayed, the artist anxiously called for him. The tiger appeared an instant later, sprang out, and padded along beside Chen-cho.

From then on, whenever he was sure they were unobserved, Chen-cho summoned Lao-hu, and the two of them wandered together, the fondest companions. When Chen-cho stopped to paint some scene or other, the tiger would stretch out next to him or disappear into the picture on some business of his own. Nevertheless, Chen-cho had only to call his name and Lao-hu would reappear immediately; and Chen-cho always kept the painting beside him when he worked.

As for his other paintings, thanks to the tiger's brush, the marvelous ink stick, and the grinding stone they became better and better, as did Chen-cho's reputation. Whenever he lodged in a town or city, he could expect any number of customers to come clamoring for his pictures. However, as always, he parted with few. Nor would he even consider selling his marvelous landscape, no matter what price was offered. So, more often than not, would-be purchasers left disappointed at being refused.

Only once did Chen-cho have a disagreeable encounter. In one town, a merchant came to inspect Chen-cho's paintings, but as soon as he saw them, he shook his head in distaste.

"What dreadful daubs are these?" he exclaimed. "Not one suitable to put in my house! And this"—he pointed at the landscape, where Lao-hu had prudently hidden himself out of sight—"worst of all! An ugly, blotchy, ill-conceived scrawl! I've had nightmares prettier than this."

Chen-cho, glad to see the merchant stamp off, flung a few tart words after him. He was, nonetheless, puzzled. He called Lao-hu, who popped out instantly.

"Easily understood," Lao-hu said, when Chen-cho told him the merchant's opinion. "As a painter, you should know this better than anyone. We see with eyes in our head, but see clearer with eyes of the heart. Some see beauty, some see ugliness. In both cases, what they see is a reflection of their own nature."

"Even so," replied Chen-cho, "a painting's a painting. Colors and shapes don't change, no matter who looks at them."

"True enough," said Lao-hu. "Very well, then, let me put it this way: You can't please everybody."

"That, I suppose," Chen-cho said, "is a blessing."

◆ ◆ ◆ ◆ ◆

While Chen-cho happily paints away with Lao-hu at his side, Jen is arriving at Chai-sang. To learn what he finds there, accompany him into the next chapter.

22

· *What Jen did not know* ·
· *What he found out* ·
· *What happened to Master Chu* ·

THERE WERE SEVERAL THINGS Jen did not know. For one, that word had spread throughout the northern province. Following Ping-erh's example, other villages stood against Natha Yellow Scarf like so many gnats and mosquitoes that he wasted no more time and effort swatting them. He turned south again, his eye on greater prizes. Jen had failed to settle accounts with his old enemy but otherwise had succeeded better than he realized.

Another thing he did not know was how, in a practical way, to find Voyaging Moon. Late one afternoon, he at last trudged into Chai-sang. He might as well have stumbled into an anthill. The streets of the provincial capital swarmed with carriages, sedan chairs, carts, barrows, and jostling passersby. It was all he could do to break free of the crowd and find a quiet spot where he could make plans, of which he had none.

Of immediate concern was still another thing he did not know: how to stay alive. He had eaten up his small store of provisions two days before. A wet snow had begun, the heavy sky threatened more, a rising wind was sharp enough to bite through the quilt around his shoulders. Following his first thought, he entered the nearest inn. No sooner did the innkeeper catch sight of this clearly unprosperous new arrival than he berated him for dripping on the clean floor. He threatened to call the watchmen if the wretch did not take himself off instantly. Jen tried to explain that he wished to work in exchange for food. The innkeeper would hear none of that. He hustled Jen into the street and promised him a number of disagreeable things if he ever again set foot inside his establishment.

Jen tried several other inns and eating houses with the same result. By this time, he could barely keep his thoughts straight. Master Hu had firmly lectured him on the virtues of honesty, but the notion floated into Jen's head that a little robbery might be unvirtuous but appropriate, and he wished he had paid more attention to Moxa.

So far, his belly had been clamoring wildly for food. Now it spoke to him calmly and reasonably.

"What could be simpler?" it said. "You have the answer in your bundle."

"The bowl?" Jen said.

"Of course," his belly replied. "Master Wu chose it as a suitable gift. Therefore, it must have value. What has value can be sold."

"The last of my offerings?" Jen protested. "I can't. Then I'd be truly empty-handed."

"Come now," said his belly, "be reasonable. When you find Voyaging Moon, as you surely will, she'll no doubt have the flute. So, you'll offer that to Yuan-ming. Assuming you reach T'ien-kuo in the first place. If you don't, then what difference will it make? Therefore, you'd be foolish to hold on to something worth a few strings of cash. More, for all you know."

Jen hesitated. His belly went on in a wheedling vein, suggesting tasty dishes and a warm bed. Jen began to suspect that his belly was very clever and subtle, with its own purposes, and not to be trusted. By now, his head was going around in circles and his knees had turned unreliable. He stumbled out of the crowd and sat down with his back against a wall.

He unwrapped the bowl and stared at it. If he chose to sell it, as his belly recommended, where could he do so? He pondered this, eyes half-closed. A voice shouted in his ear. Jen blinked up at a furious face attached to a rag-covered body.

"My corner!" the face shouted. "Get on with you. Find your own place to beg."

The man shook a heavy stick and seemed perfectly willing to crack Jen's skull with it. Instead of offering explanation or apology, Jen thought it wiser to follow the man's suggestion. He clambered up and set off down the street. Along the way, he stopped a passerby.

The man eyed the bowl in Jen's hand. "Be off! If I gave to every impudent beggar, I'd soon be one myself."

"No, no," Jen said, "to sell this—who'd buy it? Where would I go?"

"Do you take me for a pawnbroker? Well, then, go to Green Sparrow Street." The man waved impatiently and doled out directions as grudgingly as if he were handing over coins.

Jen set off accordingly. Either he had been misinformed or had misunderstood, for he found himself in a maze of alleyways. His belly continued to mutter complaints. Also, his teeth began chattering; he felt hot and cold at the same time. He picked his way through heaps of litter. He no longer remembered exactly where he had been directed. Just ahead, he caught sight of a bent figure hobbling along, leaning on a staff. Jen gave a joyful cry and ran to him.

"Master Shu!"

The old man turned. "Shu? Honorable young sir, you mistake yourself."

Jen rubbed his eyes. The man was as ragged and

grimy as Master Shu had ever been. But, indeed, he was not the old poet.

"Shu?" The aged beggar shook his head. "Not I. Chu. You seek a Master Shu but find a Master Chu. And you? Whoever you may be, I am happy to make your acquaintance. It is always a pleasure to meet a colleague.

"New to the profession, as well, if you've come to this neighborhood looking for alms." Master Chu peered into Jen's bowl. "Empty. Empty as your belly, I might guess."

"Not looking for alms," Jen said. "I want to sell this bowl. Where can I—"

"Sell your bowl?" Master Chu broke in. "Young man, a beggar without a bowl is no proper beggar at all. Why, it's your stock in trade, your trusty friend, your faithful servant. Beg well and you'll fill it with food, or a coin or two. In the course of time, what it brings you will be worth more than the little cash you'd get for it."

"Master Chu, I'm not here to beg," Jen said. "I was told that a young woman has been taken to Chai-sang. I must find her."

"Ah? That's a different matter. But, most assuredly, you will not find her. Not in your present state. You look hardly able to find your nose in the dark. Have you eaten? No? Come along, then."

Too confused and shaky to ask questions, Jen allowed Master Chu to lead him to something resembling a small shed or a large dog kennel patched together from matting and bamboo poles. Helping him inside, Master Chu rummaged through a pile of rags and torn quilts.

"I was not expecting to be honored by a guest for dinner." Master Chu unearthed a broken millet cake. He handed it to Jen. "Humblest apologies. My larder has not been overflowing these days. Eat, eat," he insisted, when Jen refused what certainly was the last of the old man's store. "By no means enough for two, but perhaps enough for one."

By this time, Jen's belly had surrendered to the assault of chills and fever. Master Chu eyed him with concern. He piled the quilts around Jen and obliged him to stretch out. "You need more than I have here," Master Chu said. "Never fear. I shall set that right."

He took the bowl from Jen's hand. "Empty, at the moment. But the usefulness of the bowl lies in its emptiness; it must be empty before it can be filled."

"Someone else said that—" Jen stared at him. "Is that you, Master Shu? Don't you know me?"

The beggar shook his head. "It is your fever speaking."

Yet, as Jen watched, for an instant the beggar's features blurred into those of the old poet. Or was it the face of Master Fu? Master Wu? All at the same time? Jen's head fell back on the pile of rags. The faces whirled before his eyes, then he saw none.

Master Chu was gone when Jen opened his eyes

again. He groped for the bowl. It, too, was gone. He cried out in dismay. He heard someone chuckle as he tried to sit up.

"Did you think I had stolen it? No, as a beggar I observe a rule of meticulous honesty." Master Chu bent over him and held out the bowl.

"As I told you," the old man said, "it must be empty before it can be filled. As it is now. Thanks to leftovers from an eating house, enough for both of us. If I have done you a service, you have done one for me.

"Unlike most of my colleagues in Chai-sang," he added, as he continued feeding Jen from the bowl, "I am not a resident beggar, but a wandering member of the profession. As for my bowl, you may well ask: Where is it? Broken, alas. Some while ago, I made a regrettable mistake in judgment. I begged alms from the one who calls himself Yellow Scarf King. As I held out my bowl to him, he struck it from my hands and smashed it under his heel. For which I was grateful, since he might have done likewise to my head. Since then, I have not been able to replace it. My takings, in consequence, have suffered—I have eaten only what my bare hands could carry. Therefore, I am glad for the use of your bowl as you, I hope, are pleased with its contents."

"Natha," Jen murmured. "Yes, Master Chu, I know his ways. He takes from prince and beggar alike."

His words went unnoticed as Master Chu kept fill-ing Jen's mouth with food. Or, if the old man did reply, Jen did not hear, having drifted back into fevered sleep.

For several days he lay half in stupor. And each day, Master Chu went out with the bowl and came back with it refilled, feeding Jen and himself from it. When Master Chu finally allowed him to sit up, Jen spoke more of Voyaging Moon and his search.

The old man shook his head. "A needle in a haystack, I fear. Chai-sang has many merchants and many young women. A flute girl? That would narrow it down a little. Difficult, nevertheless. Let me see what I can do."

"One thing more," Jen said. He had made his decision some days before, but now he put the bowl in the hands of Master Chu. "Keep this. For the sake of your kindness and your own need. If I find the one I seek, I'll have no use for it. If I do not find her, then it will make no difference to me."

Master Chu's eyes brightened. The old beggar was as delighted as if Jen had given him a dozen taels of gold, his pleasure so great that Jen felt no regret at parting from this last of his offerings. On the contrary, he felt free and lightened of the burden he had carried since leaving Ch'ang-an so long ago.

As for Master Chu, while Jen regained his strength, the old man set his plan in motion.

"I have spoken with all my colleagues," Master Chu later told him. "They know more of the goings and comings here than anyone in Chai-sang. So far, they have told me nothing of a flute girl, but they will keep eyes and ears open. They will know whom to ask and where to look. If she is here, they will find her."

Jen's hope rose. Days passed, however, with no success. Despite the efforts of the Chai-sang beggars, it was Jen himself who had word of Voyaging Moon.

It came about by accident. In addition to help from the beggars, Jen roamed the streets every day, too restless to sit and wait in Master Chu's lean-to. He hoped he might hear the sound of the flute, or perhaps be lucky enough to glimpse her at a window or passing in a carriage.

Crossing the central square one morning, he found himself jostled into a band of jugglers. Overhearing their grumbling, he gathered they had received cold welcome and were leaving the city.

"Had the flute girl been with us," one said, "it would have gone better. There was none like Voyaging Moon to fill the theater, and all our pockets."

"The name you spoke—" Jen seized the juggler's arm. The performer stared as if Jen were a maniac. "You said 'Voyaging Moon'—"

"What if I did?" The juggler tried to step aside. Jen held him fast. As he hastily poured out his account of being separated from her, the man's face softened. "Your sweetheart, eh? You're a lucky lad, then. Yes, your girl's in Nang-pei, when last I saw her, and making a fine fortune for herself."

Jen took hardly an instant to thank the juggler. He ran from one street to the next looking for Master Chu, eager to tell the news and bid him fond farewell. Jen cursed himself for not going to Nang-pei in the first place. He resolved not to lose another instant in Chai-sang. He saw nothing of the old beggar. He ran to the lean-to. It was empty. He started back toward the square. Before he reached it, he came upon one of Master Chu's colleagues, hobbling along with a crutch under his arm.

"Where's Master Chu?" Jen demanded. "I must find him quickly. There's news. Have you seen him?"

"Yes." The man's face fell. "Yes, I was there. I saw everything."

"Saw what?" Jen burst out. "What are you telling me?"

"In custody." The beggar grimaced. "He's been arrested. A grave offense."

◆　◆　◆　◆　◆

Generous, kindhearted Master Chu arrested? How can this be? What crime could he possibly have committed? Jen will find this out in the next chapter.

23

"BAD ENOUGH TO COST HIM HIS HEAD," the beggar added. "Illegal possession of royal property: a valuable bowl. He stole it, they say. Who'd have thought it of old Chu?"

Jen had heard enough. He turned and raced back to the square. He was breathless by the time he reached the Hall of Sublime Justice. Guards blocked his way at the portals. He blurted that he had important information in the matter of one Master Chu, that he must speak to the officials in charge.

"Witness?" a guard said. "Not that one's needed. Go in, then, for whatever it is you have to testify."

Jen flung himself past the guards and into the Chamber of Truthful Testimonies, fearing he might be too late or that Master Chu had been taken elsewhere. He cried out in relief. The hearing was still in progress. Master Chu, with two burly attendants flanking him, was on his knees before the magistrate's heavily carved desk.

Heads turned as Jen pushed through clerks and court officers. At the sight of him, Master Chu's face wrinkled in dismay and his lips tried to shape a silent warning.

"Never fear," Jen murmured. He halted beside the old beggar and faced the official he took to be the prosecutor, firmly declaring, "The accusation is false. I swear to that. There is injustice—"

"Hold your tongue." The official looked Jen up and down coldly. "You have just come into this honorable court. What do you know of the accusation to call it false? Justice has not been delivered. Therefore, how dare you call it unjust?"

"An accusation of theft—" Jen began.

"A charge I myself laid against this criminal," the prosecutor snapped. "I passed him in the street not two hours ago. I observed the bowl he held out. With a trained eye for such rare objects of art, I recognized it as valuable. Too valuable to be in a beggar's hands. When I examined it, I saw the dragon emblem on the bottom. Only royal property bears that mark. Thus the correct conclusion is that it is stolen. What possible testimony can you add?"

"I can add that he didn't steal it—"

"Let him speak, first, in his own defense," broke in the official. "Why does he refuse, as the record shows?"

At a sign from the prosecutor, the court scribe read aloud from a page of notes:

"Questioned as to possession of stolen object, accused states he was given it by a friend. Asked to name that individual, he stated that he refused to do so."

The prosecutor shrugged. "The reason is obvious. He refuses to say who gave it to him because he himself stole it. A pitiful attempt to trick the court. The accusation stands. The case is clear."

"It is, indeed. I am quite satisfied," said the magistrate. Until now, he had been bent over the bowl, studying it closely. He set it down in front of him and raised his head. "There is no possibility that a beggar has come by this honestly."

Jen stifled a gasp. He found himself looking into a heavy-jowled, toadlike face. Suddenly the memory flashed into his mind—the official who had ordered him beaten, who had arrogantly declared his rank and destination: Official of the First Rank, Chief Magistrate of Chai-sang, Honorable Fat-choy.

For his part, Fat-choy gave no sign of recognition. He yawned, tapped his fan, and gestured impatiently. "What further testimony? You come as witness?

To this thief's good character? One villain to praise another?"

Fat-choy glanced around. The court officials giggled dutifully at his show of wit. He nodded and went on. "The law requires me to hear you. It does not require me to hear you in perpetuity. Speak up quickly. Waste no more of the court's precious time, or mine."

"This man told the truth," Jen replied. "He did not steal the bowl. I gave it to him."

"Ah? Did you?" Fat-choy raised his eyebrows. "I compliment you on such magnificent generosity, one of the Eleven Principal Virtues. Logic now compels me to inquire where, in turn, you obtained it. Perhaps from some other mysterious, unnameable friend?"

Master Chu wrung his hands. "Fool, fool," he whispered. "I tried to warn you to keep silent. Do you mean to dig your own grave? I am so close to mine it hardly matters. Oh, you should have let well enough alone."

"It will be easily settled." Jen gave him a reassuring smile. He looked squarely at Fat-choy. "The bowl is, in fact, royal property from King T'ai's Hall of Priceless Treasures. It was put in my charge. You shall prove the truth of this by sending word to the Celestial Palace in Ch'ang-an.

"Until you receive a message confirming what I have told you," Jen continued, "I accept being kept in custody here, wherever you choose to confine me.

"One thing more." For the first time in many

months, Jen spoke aloud and clearly his rank and name. "I am the Young Lord Prince. I am Jen Shao-yeh."

The prosecutor's jaw dropped. "But—but this is hardly credible. You? As you claim—yes, that can be proved. Be certain that an inquiry will be dispatched immediately to the Celestial Palace. Until then—"

"No need," broke in Fat-choy. From the moment that Jen named himself, the official's eyes lit up in sudden recollection.

"I know this man," Fat-choy declared. "Prince? Yes. Prince of Robbers. He and his band assaulted me on my way here. They stole horses, carts, provisions. Even then, to confuse me and distract my attention, he pretended to be the Young Lord. Now he offers new trickery. Put himself in custody? Live at public expense to further some devious plan of his own?"

Jen's eyes flashed. "Have a care, Official of the First Rank Fat-choy. You deal with a royal personage. Your conduct will be noted—"

"Silence!" shouted Fat-choy. "Impudent liar! You dare to speak of my conduct? Insolence on top of insolence! Do you think you can employ some clever ruse and brazen your way out of punishment?" Fat-choy struck his fist on the desk. "Another word, villain, and you shall be bound and gagged." He turned to Master Chu, who was staring openmouthed at Jen.

"As for you," Fat-choy declared, "there is no longer a case against you. This wretch has confessed to possessing and transmitting stolen property. Knowing him as I do, I willingly believe he gave you the bowl, no doubt to rid himself of incriminating evidence. Since you are innocent, I shall only have you flogged out of Chai-sang. Set foot here again and you will pay with your head."

Fat-choy motioned to the attendants, who dragged the bewildered and protesting Master Chu from the Hall of Sublime Justice. Two guards came forward to lay hands on Jen.

"Your case is more difficult," said Fat-choy, fixing a bulging eye on Jen, "but you shall have justice nonetheless, impartial, guided by the law, which is more than you deserve.

"First," he continued, "in the matter of your robbery and attack on an official, I would gladly punish you to the full extent. However, your vicious assault took place beyond my present jurisdiction. It cannot figure here and, regretfully, I must set it aside.

"In the matter of the bowl, you have condemned yourself out of your own mouth. This is a capital crime. The punishment is beheading.

"And yet," Fat-choy went on, as Jen stared horrified, "much as you merit the extreme penalty, the law forbids it. Because you have made voluntary confession, I am required by statute to mitigate your sentence and to show you clemency. Which I now do. Your life is mercifully spared."

Jen heaved a sigh of relief. Then his blood froze as the official continued. "Instead of a death sentence, by the benevolence and compassion of the law, you shall wear the Collar of Punishment."

Fat-choy motioned to the guards. "Take him to the public square immediately. Set the cangue around his neck."

"Chief Magistrate." Jen looked straight at Fat-choy. Whatever else, he would give the chief magistrate no further satisfaction. With the princely bearing he had learned from Master Hu, he said, "Your judgment is incorrect. It is also incomplete. You have not specified the length of sentence."

Fat-choy smiled. "It is not given to mortals, or to this court, to know precisely how many years one may live. For you, what that number may be, such will be the duration."

◆　◆　◆　◆　◆

Gross injustice! Will Jen escape the dreadful punishment of the cangue? Before that is answered, we leave him being dragged to the public square and turn our attention to Fat-choy in the next chapter.

24

· *The Tale of the Bronze Bowl* ·

HONORABLE CHIEF MAGISTRATE, Official of the First Rank Fat-choy admired himself as a personage of refined taste and delicate sensibilities. He wore robes of exquisite materials richly embroidered. If he judged his meals to be less than perfect, he flung the dishes to the floor and ordered his cook beaten to perfection. His chambers were filled with superb antiques, pieces of jade, porcelain, gold, and silver, and he sought always to add rare items to his collection.

When a bronze bowl was presented as evidence in a

case of theft, Honorable Fat-choy's eyes popped and his fingers itched. To one of less perception, it would have seemed a common object. Honorable Fat-choy, however, saw its subtle decorations, graceful proportions, and excellent craftsmanship. He was more than a little vexed that Honorable Prosecutor Ch'iang-to had seen it first. The conceited fellow thought himself also a connoisseur. Fat-choy thought him a fool.

"Had it been me," Fat-choy muttered, "I'd have simply taken it away from the beggar who was holding it—the wretch wouldn't have dared to complain—or given him a few coins and said no more. But no, this idiot makes a court case of the matter. Now the thing turns out to be royal property. By law, it must be sent back to the Celestial Palace."

Fat-choy pondered the situation and soon found an answer.

"True, the law requires me to return the bowl. On the other hand, it does not specify how quickly this must be done. That leaves it to the discretion, honesty, and efficiency of the chief magistrate, who, fortunately, is myself. A heavy responsibility, but I am capable of bearing it."

Fat-choy, therefore, ordered the bowl placed in his chambers along with his other prized possessions.

Honorable Prosecutor Ch'iang-to ventured to raise a question. "Most worthy and excellent Chief Magistrate, since the bowl figured as evidence in a criminal trial, until it can be sent back to its rightful owner, in my considered opinion it should remain in custody of the Department of Legal Technicalities."

"Of which you, most admirably diligent Honorable Prosecutor, are the head," replied Fat-choy. "However, since the case has been judged and closed, the bowl comes under the purview of the Department of Vigilant Administration."

"Of which you, Honorable Fat-choy, are the head," answered the prosecutor.

"Correct," replied Fat-choy, "and, may I point out, your superior in rank. In my considered opinion, the times are too unsettled to return the bowl immediately. Harm might come to it in transport over bandit-infested roads. What safer place, for the moment, than my private chambers, where I may constantly keep an eye on it?"

Honorable Ch'iang-to could only bow agreement. Fat-choy waddled off to his quarters. He had, that day, ordered an old beggar whipped out of town, condemned a thieving impostor to the Collar of Punishment, imprisoned half a dozen rogues to prevent them from committing offenses they might have contemplated in the future, and decided in favor of litigants who had impressed him with the righteousness of their purses and their generosity in sharing the contents with him, and he was altogether fatigued by dispensing so much justice.

He enjoyed a delicious dinner, allowed a servant to anoint him with fragrant essence of rose petals, and spent the rest of the evening fondling his collection of treasures.

He set the bowl in a place of honor on a teakwood stand. The more he studied his new acquisition, the more he admired it, and the more he congratulated himself on his dealing with Honorable Ch'iang-to.

"What a distasteful example of greed," Fat-choy said. "He had the notion of dishonestly keeping it for himself. Well, here it is, here it stays. Sooner or later, one of these years, I shall return it. If I remember to do so."

Fat-choy went happily to sleep. Next morning, like a child with a new toy, he hurried over to inspect this latest item in his collection. He had to look three times before he believed his eyes.

The bowl held a gold coin.

"Well, well, well," said Fat-choy, picking up the coin. He squinted at it, rubbed it between his fingers, bit it, rapped it on the tabletop. It was genuine, of purest gold. "I don't remember dropping this into the bowl last night. Yet so I must have done without thinking about it."

Fat-choy slipped the coin into the purse at his belt and went about his daily duties. That evening, returning to his chambers, he went to admire the bowl again.

Two gold coins lay in the bottom.

Fat-choy rubbed his jowls and blinked his eyes. This time, he was sure he had not absentmindedly dropped money into the bowl.

"Ah, now I understand," he said. "My servants found these on the floor while cleaning my room. Yes, I must have dropped the coins. They rolled into some corner, my servants discovered them and put them where I would be sure to see."

Satisfied by his analysis, he attacked his dinner with a keen appetite and went to sleep.

In the morning, the bowl held four gold coins.

This bewildered Fat-choy and made him a little uneasy. Someone must have come into his chamber while he slept. Again, he turned his mind to solving the mystery, which now seemed a highly profitable one.

"Of course," he finally said to himself, "now it becomes clear. Someone, plaintiff or defendant, has a case coming up for judgment. These coins are tokens of his respect and good will. They indicate justice is on his side. In the course of time, this righteous individual will make himself known. Meanwhile, he has asked one of my servants to bestow this money on me discreetly."

To prove this, he called in his servants. All replied they knew nothing of such a petitioner. Fat-choy sent them away and went back to unraveling the mystery.

"Simple explanation," he said. "They are lying. All in a good cause, and I forgive them. This unknown personage has ordered them to keep the matter secret. All will be revealed in proper time."

That evening, when Fat-choy returned to his chambers, he saw the bowl held eight coins.

"Now at last I understand," he cried in delight. "At

first, I thought it must be some litigant or favor-seeker. But they would be bolder and blunter and take up the matter with me directly. No, this is a graceful, elegant, feminine way of going at things.

"Yes, a lady is involved," he went on, preening himself, "a lady of wealth. Beauty, surely, to go with it. She has observed me about town or in the Hall of Sublime Justice and has quite lost her heart. She wishes, naturally, to remain unknown for a while, to see what I shall do. Perhaps it is a little humorous game to find out if I can discover who she is. That might be difficult, for there must be countless rich and beautiful ladies filled with tender emotions for me."

Next morning, the bowl held sixteen gold coins.

Fat-choy hugged himself gleefully. "Ah, flirtatious minx! How she must enjoy the riddle she sets me!

"If this is a little game," he continued, "two can play at it. I have already established that someone is tiptoeing in during the night. A servant or, perhaps, the lady herself, who has bribed her way into the yamen. Very well, I shall go to bed as usual, but only pretend to be sleeping. At the sound of someone entering, I shall spring up and surprise whoever it is."

Despite his efforts, he could not keep himself awake all night.

When he opened his eyes, he saw thirty-two gold coins in the bowl.

"How did she do it?" he cried. "To creep in so quietly, with never a sound?"

The following night, Fat-choy bolted his door, thinking this might cause the unknown admirer to change her method and make herself known.

Next morning, he found sixty-four gold pieces.

The following days, each time Fat-choy left his chambers he returned to find double the previous amount. He tried sitting up all night watching the bowl. However, when he glanced away even for a moment, still more coins had appeared when he looked back.

"Finally, I understand!" he joyfully exclaimed. "Why did I not realize it from the beginning? This fortune is no gift from favor-seeker or admirer.

"Celestial providence is showering me with gold! A reward for my honesty and diligence, for my generosity and nobility of spirit, for my wise dispensation of justice.

"Yes, I have read tales of kindly spirits rewarding mortals worthy of such benevolence. And who could be worthier than I? I never believed those tales, but here is proof."

With the amount continually doubling, the gold coins soon overflowed the capacity of the bowl, covered the table, and spilled onto the floor. Fat-choy piled the coins into his cabinet and locked the bowl there as well.

But the cabinet itself became filled. Fat-choy began wondering where else he could store this multiplying treasure.

"No telling when it will stop," he said to himself. "Perhaps it never will! Indeed, why should it?"

He needed no abacus to calculate he would shortly become rich beyond imagination. His head spun at the prospect of dozens of gorgeous carriages and teams of horses, of thousands of new robes, luxurious furnishings, priceless objects of art, residences to house them all; as well as gardens, orchards, pavilions. Each day, he could hardly wait to return to his chambers and peep into the overflowing cabinet.

At this time, there arrived in Chai-sang Honorable Inspector General Tso-tsang. It was the duty of this high official to examine account books and ledgers, to conduct investigations, perform inventories, and verify all expenses connected with yamens throughout the kingdom.

Fat-choy was too preoccupied with counting his growing treasure to give more than briefly formal welcome to this visiting official and paid no heed to his doings. Later, when Fat-choy opened his chamber door to insistent knocking, he saw Inspector General Tso-tsang in company with Honorable Prosecutor Ch'iang-to.

"Forgive this intrusion, Honorable Chief Magistrate," said the Inspector General as the impatient Fat-choy ushered them in, "but a question has arisen in regard to certain accounts and inventories."

"It is your worthy function to deal with it," replied Fat-choy. "I am concerned with duties more important than counting bushels of rice and adding up kitchen expenses."

"It is a little more serious than that," the Inspector General said. "As required, I personally examined the strong room where reserves of currency are kept."

"Excellent," said Fat-choy. "I am happy to know that you are carrying out your duties so meticulously. Now, if you will excuse me."

"Honorable Fat-choy," said the Inspector General, "I discovered something highly troubling. In fact, disastrous. Every sack of gold coins stored there is empty."

"What?" cried Fat-choy. "How can that be? Quite impossible. Honorable Tso-tsang, you must get to the bottom of this incredible situation immediately."

"As I have been doing," replied Tso-tsang. "It is obviously the work of a most audacious robber, one within the yamen itself. No other could have access to the strong room."

"Of course it is," replied Fat-choy. "Every servant, every official, from lowest to highest, must be closely questioned." He glanced sharply at Ch'iang-to. "Including the Honorable Prosecutor himself."

"I am happy that you agree," said the Inspector General. "I have already conducted such an investigation, to no avail."

"Then probe deeper," said Fat-choy. "I urge you to do so without delay."

"Your encouragement is commendable," said the Inspector General. "That is exactly why I have come to you. So far, all officials, including the Honorable Prosecutor, have allowed me to search their chambers. I have no doubt that you, Honorable Chief Magistrate, will do likewise. Purely as a gesture of good faith and token of enthusiastic cooperation.

"The sooner we begin," Tso-tsang went on, "the sooner this inconvenient formality will be ended. Shall we, then, start with . . . oh, let us say, with your cabinet? A handsome piece of furniture, I hasten to add. I offer compliments on your taste."

"But—but this is unseemly! It impugns my dignity! It—it is outrageous!" Fat-choy had broken into a cold sweat. He scowled and glared, with as bold a face as he could put on. He blustered, protested, and, finally, folding his arms, refused to submit to such humiliation.

"In that case," replied the Inspector General, "I must take other measures."

He clapped his hands and a number of clerks and scribes entered. At his bidding, while Fat-choy gasped and sputtered, they broke open the cabinet.

Coins flooded out in a golden stream. Fat-choy collapsed on a chair. The Inspector General turned a severe eye on the Chief Magistrate.

"With utmost courtesy, allow me to inquire how you came by such bounty?"

"Gifts! Gifts!" cried Fat-choy. "Gifts from kindly spirits!"

The Inspector General and the Honorable Prosecutor exchanged glances. The clerks and scribes set about counting the coins. When they finished, the sum tallied exactly with the amount of missing treasure.

"Honorable Chief Magistrate, Official of the First Rank Fat-choy," said Prosecutor Ch'iang-to, smiling blissfully, "it is my painful duty to place you under arrest."

Fat-choy, thereupon, was put under guard and hustled into the Hall of Sublime Justice. He was forced to kneel before his own desk and his own chair, occupied now by the Inspector General, legally empowered to sit as judge in such extreme cases.

"The bowl!" blurted Fat-choy, when permitted to speak in his defense. "The kindly spirits put coins into it each day! The bowl filled more and more with gold. I had nothing whatever to do with it. Prove it for yourself. Take the bowl. Put it in your chamber. Go to sleep. See what it holds next morning."

"The bowl in question," said the Inspector General, "an item of royal property, which should have been immediately returned to the Celestial Palace, was in your custody. It cannot be found. This is yet another breach of your responsibilities."

"Gone?" burst out Fat-choy. "The kindly spirits have taken it away!"

"My reply," said the Honorable Prosecutor, "is a simple one. Never in all my career have I heard such a pitiful and ridiculous explanation, and the most barefaced, preposterous lie that any arrant criminal has ever invented. Even more preposterous than the thief who recently claimed to be the Young Lord Prince."

"I have heard enough," said the Inspector General. "Under the law, I have authority to condemn you to death. But the law is merciful as well as just. I must take into account the fact that every coin has been retrieved. The bowl alone is missing, but I charitably presume it will eventually be found. Also, I must consider that you are—or were—a colleague, and professional courtesy has certain obligations. Therefore, I pronounce a compassionate and lenient sentence upon you."

Accordingly, Fat-choy was stripped of his rank, his position, and his belongings, including his collection of antiques, and was flung out the gates of his former yamen. All his rich garments had been forfeited, but he was permitted to keep one cotton undershirt.

Fat-choy, reduced to being a beggar, proved a most unpopular one. He constantly whined, moaned, and ranted about his former wealth and his cruel betrayal by malicious spirits. Some good-hearted soul had given him an earthen pot as a begging bowl, but he seldom filled it, for passersby paid him little heed and for the most part brushed him aside.

As for the bronze bowl, a thorough search of the yamen failed to discover it. As far as could be determined, it had vanished beyond recovery and the case was closed.

One morning, however, an old beggar hobbled to a riverbank near Chai-sang. Amid the reeds and cattails, he glimpsed an object half sunk in the mud.

"Ah, so there you are," said Master Chu.

He bent and picked up the bronze bowl, examined it carefully and nodded with satisfaction. Then, clutching his find, he tottered off as quickly as his frail legs could carry him.

◆ ◆ ◆ ◆ ◆

Leaving the miserable Fat-choy in the streets of Chai-sang, and Master Chu holding the last of Jen's gifts, we now return to Jen himself and what happens to him in the next chapter.

25

· Jen contemplates his situation ·
· Interesting device ·
· War against Master Cangue ·

MASTER HU HAD ONCE REMARKED that everything was interesting if looked at carefully. Jen applied this observation to his present circumstances. First, he put Chai-sang out of his thoughts. He admitted that he had not entirely behaved with the dignity and noble fortitude Master Hu would have liked. In fact, when the Administrator of Benevolent Correction bolted and sealed the wooden collar, Jen was raging and kicking and had to be held down. Sent stumbling through the streets, goaded past the outskirts of town, he gladly took refuge in the empty countryside. He hoped somehow to meet Master Chu. The old beggar might be hiding in the underbrush, waiting for a safe moment to appear. This did not happen. Jen, therefore, set about finding a way to free himself and to calmly analyze what he had to deal with. Master Hu had been correct. Considered as object—aside from being fastened around his neck—the cangue, in its own way, was interesting.

At first glance, it was only a simple piece of wood with a hole in it. On one side, hinges allowed the device to swing open like jaws, and then snap shut around the victim's neck. But, as he discovered, it was heavy. The muscles of his shoulders already ached a little. The weight of the cangue slowed his steps and caused him to walk with a stoop. This posture strained his back and tired his legs. If he tried to walk quickly, his breath grew shallow and labored. When he sat down to rest, if he bowed his head the collar pressed against his upper legs. To lie flat was difficult, for his neck was forced to bend awkwardly. It was interesting that a mere plank could be so uncomfortable.

Its size and proportions were also interesting. The collar was quite wide. His arms, no matter how he stretched them, could not encompass it. His hands could not touch his head. His mouth lay beyond the reach of his fingers. He put aside the problem of how to feed himself. He had, in any case, nothing to eat. He turned his attention to breaking free.

Master Hu had always urged him, in his studies, to

go to the heart of the problem. Here, the heart of the problem was a thick iron rod. Clamped on the unhinged edge of the collar, it served as a bolt to keep the device firmly closed. If he could pry loose this bolt or somehow shatter it, the collar would swing open. How to accomplish this would require careful analysis.

"Master Cangue," Jen said, "whoever devised you did it cleverly and neatly." He had once held a conversation with his belly, so it seemed not too extraordinary to hold a conversation with a piece of wood. "To undo you, I must be equally clever."

The cangue did not answer.

"Very well," Jen said. "To business."

Thus began his war with the cangue.

He scuffed through dry leaves. His foot soon struck what he wanted: a rock large enough to serve his purpose, but not so heavy that he could not handle it. He knelt and groped to pry it from the frozen ground. He had to apply some effort, but at last it came out like a loose tooth. He hefted it, satisfied.

With all his might, he struck at the bolt. The rock glanced off the bar. Unable to see his target, he had not struck it squarely. He recalculated and hammered at the bolt again. The iron rang dully. The impact of the blow jarred his head and neck. He continued, nevertheless. He heard a crack. Something had broken. It was not the bolt. The rock had split in his hand. He threw the fragments aside.

"You are stubborn," he said.

The cangue said nothing.

It took him some time to find another suitable hammer. He set about pounding at the bolt again. With the weight of the cangue and the difficulty of striking at something he could not see, he was quickly out of breath, sweating despite the cold. His arm grew weary, his muscles lost their strength.

He understood. The cangue, in its own sly way, was trying to exhaust him. He could not allow that.

He sat on the ground until his strength came back. He began again. Sometimes he struck heavy blows, sometimes he tapped and chipped at the bolt. He believed that if he hit at the proper angle he would find its weak spot.

His persistence was rewarded. Another blow and the iron rod dropped at his feet. Jen gave a cry of triumph.

The cangue did not open.

This puzzled him. Then, from the corner of his eye he glimpsed what he had overlooked. The cangue was cleverer than he had supposed.

There were two more iron rods. They were affixed to the front of the collar on either side of the hole. He could not reach them.

He forced himself to stay calm. The cangue had lured him into believing it was a simple matter of breaking a single bolt. He had worn himself out uselessly. He would have to reconsider his situation.

He clung to reason and logic. He could not break all the bolts. Therefore, he must break the collar.

He set off through the woodlands, casting around until he saw what he required. Two trees had grown close together, the slender trunks nearly touching. There was room enough; he could wedge the cangue between them. This would give him the leverage he needed. If he applied enough force, the collar would split. Accordingly, he thrust one side of the cangue into the angle where the trunks nearly joined. He twisted back and forth and pressed all his weight against the collar.

The cangue did not yield. He fell back, gasping from his exertions. His strength was working against itself. His neck would snap instead of the collar.

He began to tremble. His head spun, his thoughts tumbled over each other. Throwing aside reason and logic, he desperately battered the cangue against the trees. He stumbled back, then ran headlong, plunging between the forking trunks. He cried out in pain as the cangue bit into his collarbone and wrenched his shoulder.

Somewhere in his mind, a little frightened animal began to scurry back and forth. Its name was panic. He threw himself blindly against the tree trunks until his whole body screamed with pain. He seized the edges of the cangue. By sheer strength he tried to rip the thing from his neck. The cangue tore his skin and turned it slippery with blood.

For the first time, he had to consider the one possibility he had refused to admit: that he could not free himself. Little by little, the full horror of his plight dawned on him. It was as if the cangue had foreseen his every effort and had known in advance each attempt he would make. It had patiently waited, allowing him to match wits and strength against it, to fling himself back and forth, to roll on the ground, twisting and turning. And it was still there.

The cangue had been silent, as though observing Jen's struggles with amusement. Now it spoke close to his ear:

"Did you not suppose every prisoner has done likewise? How foolish to think you might succeed where others failed. Understand one thing. There is no escape from me. I am Master Cangue."

The cangue said no more. If it did, Jen did not hear. He had thrown back his head and was howling like a wolf.

* * * * *

What hope is left? In the grip of the cangue, what can Jen do? Is there any possibility of ridding himself of this monstrous device? These questions, as well as other matters, are taken up in the next chapter.

26

• *Stern teacher* •
• *Marvelous dreams* •
• *Reflections in a puddle* •

IT SNOWED THAT NIGHT. By morning, black branches
turned sparkling white. Bare hillsides were dazzlingly
blanketed. Snow collected in dry, rocky valleys that
now looked like so many gleaming lakes. The sky
cleared to rich blue, dabbed here and there with pink.
An orange sun floated low on the horizon. A landscape
worthy of the painter Chen-cho.

The prisoner of the cangue had spent the night
crouched in a bush. He had not slept well. He had not,
in fact, slept at all, except for the occasional moment

when his head dropped and his chin rested on the wooden collar. The skin of his neck, where the collar gripped, had been torn in the course of his struggles. The blood had clotted, or frozen; the collar fretted away the scabby crust, biting into exposed flesh. The prisoner of the cangue ignored this discomfort. The animal panic of the day before had gone into its burrow, having worn itself out. The prisoner of the cangue was reasonably calm. He had much to do.

He crawled out. He could not stand upright. His spine and his knees seemed to have bent and frozen stiff. He limped from the woodlands and crossed snowy fields, trying to kick away the cramps in his legs. He bore northward, away from Chai-sang. Later in the morning, he struck what he was looking for: a fairly good road that would lead him in the general direction of Nang-pei. He had given up the prospect of reaching T'ien-kuo. Not entirely given it up. It hung somewhere in the shadows of his mind. It simply no longer had any great importance. He concentrated on finding a flute girl and, meantime, getting free of the cangue.

Country folk were on the road. Some trudged beside ox carts or pushed barrows. They were on their way to market in Chai-sang or some neighboring village. The bright morning had put them in good spirits. Children frolicked beside their elders, shouting and tossing snowballs. The sudden appearance of the prisoner caused uneasiness. The straggling procession of carts and barrows veered aside, giving him wide berth.

Several of the folk stared curiously. Most kept their eyes fixed straight ahead.

The prisoner of the cangue had given further thought to his condition. He accepted one fact: He had no means of breaking himself from the collar. He must find means. The prisoner observed the passersby. He singled out a bluff, hearty-looking fellow who laughed and joked with his companions.

The prisoner of the cangue approached him, making friendly gestures. The banter stopped. The man's friends, silent, glanced at each other and edged away.

The prisoner asked for something to pry open the cangue.

"I do anything like that," the man retorted, "I'll end up with one of those on my own neck. I'm sorry for you, but that's as far as it goes. Be on your way."

The prisoner wondered if he should identify himself. He decided it would be useless. Instead, he repeated his request for tools.

"None here," the man said. "Be off, I told you."

"You have an ax." The prisoner pointed at a heap of oddments in the cart.

"There is no ax."

"I see one. Give it here."

"There is no ax."

The man turned away. The prisoner followed, insistent. The man warned him to keep his distance. The prisoner pushed past him and tried to lay hands on the implement. Alarmed, the man cursed and shoved him aside. The prisoner was stubborn. He lunged toward the cart, swinging the edge of his collar against the man, who was now frightened. He stepped ahead of the prisoner and seized an ox goad. He brandished the iron-tipped pole.

"Enough of that. Get away."

The prisoner would not be denied. He started once more for the cart. The man struck him with the ox goad. The prisoner reeled back, regained his balance, and tried to snatch the pole. The man understood that he was dealing with a dangerous criminal. He brought the ox goad down on the prisoner's head. The prisoner fell. The man pondered whether to strike again. He judged it unnecessary. He set off with his cart as quickly as the ox could go.

The prisoner had been thoroughly stunned. By the time he got his wits back, the country folk were too far down the road to be overtaken. He started north again. He did not feel kindly disposed toward those folk. He halted. By the roadside, someone had set a pile of broken victuals. The prisoner flung himself on the bits of food. He could not put them into his mouth. On all fours, he devoured them where they lay.

At this point, the prisoner had worn the cangue less than two days.

It snowed often that winter. Bad weather forced the prisoner to go at a snail's pace. Sometimes he lost his bearings amid the whirlwind of white flakes. Once, in the weeks that followed, he went in a large circle, ending where he had begun.

The cangue did not speak to him again. It was, nevertheless, an excellent teacher—stern and demanding, but always fair. As long as the prisoner did what the cangue required, they got on well enough. The cangue taught him many useful things: how to lap water like an animal; how to sleep sitting up; how to walk half bent—the prisoner found a staff to help him do so.

The cangue also taught him to avoid towns and villages when possible, to enter them only if absolutely necessary. The prisoner was not welcome there; his presence made the inhabitants uncomfortable and they sometimes drove him off with sticks. So the cangue taught him to shelter in peasants' outbuildings and to be quiet about it and not approach the dwellings. With the same instinct that told them a fox or wolf roamed their fields, the farm folk knew he was there. Some chased him away, but most ignored his presence. As often as not, they set out food for him. The cangue taught him to crouch over it and gulp it down before other stray creatures snatched it from him.

The cangue rewarded him for learning such lessons. It granted him marvelous dreams. Asleep, the prisoner was deliriously happy, his dreams so bright, so real that he was often confused when he woke. He could not be certain whether he was a prisoner dreaming of happiness, or a happy man dreaming he was a prisoner. Someone had once told him something like that. He could not remember who or when.

The cangue rewarded him, as well, by allowing him to lose track of time. The prisoner at first counted the days. So many accumulated that they became as heavy as the wooden collar. The cangue permitted him to forget such details. It was either dark or light, snowing or not snowing, he had either eaten or had not. This relieved him of painfully calculating how long he had been on the roads.

One day, he grew vaguely aware of a greenish cast to the landscape, a green thickening among trees and hedges, rain instead of snow, mud instead of frozen turf. This pleased him.

The sun had grown noticeably warmer by the time he reached Nang-pei. He had been ill and feverish, but his spirits lifted and he felt a joyful excitement until now confined to his dreams. He made his way cautiously into the town, to the thieves' and beggars' quarter, which the cangue had taught him to sniff out unerringly.

He singled out a possible source of information: a street urchin, a ragged boy with a shrewd look on his narrow face. The prisoner beckoned. The boy swaggered over, grinning, studying the collar around the prisoner's neck as if he himself expected to wear one someday and wished a close look at what lay in store.

The prisoner inquired if he knew of a certain flute girl, a performer at the theater.

"Who doesn't?" The boy put his hands on his hips. "Lady Shadow Behind a Screen."

The prisoner did not recognize that name. From the

boy's added description, he knew who it must be. He asked how to send her a message.

"You and a hundred others." The boy chuckled. "Can't be done."

The prisoner replied that it must be done.

"Can't," the urchin repeated. "One good reason: She's gone. That's right. In a great carriage. We lined the streets to wave. We were sorry to see her go. Where? No idea. North? South? East? West? It would have to be one of them, wouldn't it?

"Here, now, old uncle," the boy added, rapping sharply on the front of the cangue, "don't go to sleep."

The prisoner had not gone to sleep. He had merely shut his eyes and let his head drop forward. He could barely absorb what the urchin told him. The boy waited a few moments. The prisoner did not move. The boy wondered if he had died. He shrugged and went off whistling down the street.

The prisoner dimly understood he would have to think what next to do. To begin, he must leave Nangpei. He hoped some thoughts would come to him by the time he reached the outskirts. None did. He sat down by the roadside. A strange new creature had roused inside his head; he glimpsed it lurking in the shadows.

Children played nearby, splashing in the puddles. They sidled up to the prisoner. He wished to tell them that their parents would be distressed and angry to see them loitering around him. But his tongue had grown thick and unmanageable, and he could not shape his words. He gestured them away. The children were not afraid. They observed him with interest. One cheerfully asked what crime he had committed. A girl held up a rice cake she had been munching. Did he want it? She stepped closer and put the cake into his mouth, grinning proudly, as if she had dared something highly dangerous.

Since the prisoner only sat motionless and showed no sign of doing anything exciting, the children grew bored and drifted away. The prisoner, actually, was very busy with the new animal. It was not panic, not love, fear, anger, hatred, or anything he had known. It had sharp claws and sharp teeth.

The prisoner had developed a raging thirst. Leaving the beast crouching in his mind, he lurched to one of the puddles and bent over it. He did not drink. A face stared up at him. The hair was long and matted, the nose and brow almost black, the skin flaked and peeling. It reminded him of someone. He racked his memory. Finally, it struck him.

"Where have you been?" he cried. "Master Shu!"

He reached out to embrace the old man. The animal, despair, took advantage of this moment of inattention. It leaped and sank its teeth.

* * * * *

Must a journey that began so brightly come to such an end? Jen has lost hope; will he survive without it? For the answer, turn to the next chapter.

27

· Two prosperous merchants ·
· Fortune changes for the better ·
· Or for the worse? ·

THIS DREAM WAS DIFFERENT. It was not as marvelous as the others. It kept breaking into bits and disappearing. People he did not know floated in and out. He felt as if he had been wrapped up, unable to move. Sometimes his mouth was opened and things put into it, which he chewed and swallowed instinctively. Most of the timeless time, he drifted through lightless corridors. As always, in his dreams, he wore no wooden collar. That was good. Otherwise, disappointing. He had hoped for something brighter. He had hoped to meet Voyaging Moon, as he so often did.

Eventually, he could see more clearly. Here were two gentlemen, both well-dressed. They could have been prosperous merchants. They looked vaguely familiar. One had a round, lumpy face; the other was lean, with long, ropy hair. It took him a while to recognize them.

"Mafoo? Moxa?" Jen said. "In handsome new clothes? What a fine dream this is turning out to be."

"Call me a dream, eh?" Mafoo slapped his large and solid belly. "Here's reality, well-stuffed. I got back better than I lost. You're awake, be sure of that."

Moxa came to the bedside. "If you think you're dreaming, what do you say to this?" He held up something in front of Jen. "Go on, touch it. See for yourself."

It was the cangue, shattered.

"I cracked it open," Moxa said proudly. "Good thing no one saw me, or we'd all have been in trouble."

Jen took the collar in his hands. He passed his fingers over the splintered wood and broken bolts. He looked up at Mafoo and Moxa.

"No dream," Jen murmured. "I'm free of it." For the first time since he had worn the collar, he wept with joy.

"You'll tell us later how you got yourself into such a plight." Mafoo gently put a hand on Jen's shoulder. "The main thing is that you're out. Give that monstrosity here. I'll get rid of it now."

"I'll keep it," Jen said. "If I ever wonder if this is

still a dream, all I need to do is look at it. And at the two of you. My dear friends, how did you find me? And where am I?"

"Specifically," the Mad Robber said, "we found you in a mud puddle. Generally, you're in Nang-pei—at the best inn available, you'll be pleased to know. You've been sick a good while. We've had doctors coming and going, stuffing pills and potions down your gullet, and servants feeding you between times. You were far gone; we feared you mightn't come back."

"We've been trying to catch up with you for months," added Mafoo. "We lost track of you at the beginning of winter. Moxa picked up your trail again a few weeks ago."

"By the Ear of Continual Attentiveness!" exclaimed the Mad Robber. "It never fails. Talk, rumors, gossip. Some grateful villagers in a backwater called Ping-erh remembered you well. Ah, if only we'd found you before this."

"We did the best we could," Mafoo said. "I and this skinny madman," he added, with an affectionate grin at Moxa, "got swept beyond the mouth of the Lo, almost out to sea. We hung on for dear life to what was left of the boat. It took some doing to paddle back. We must have saved each other's life half a dozen times. We made shore at last and started upriver on foot. We sheltered in a fisherman's hut. He told us about a young fellow—we guessed it was you—who might have headed for Chen-yeh."

"No sign of you there," Moxa put in, "but the Ear of Continual Attentiveness heard of a flute girl who'd been at the Golden Grasshopper long before. We talked to the proprietor, a disagreeable creature."

"And got nothing from him," Jen said bitterly.

"On the contrary," Moxa said. "We got a great deal. On the Feet of Stealthy Silence, I went back that night and robbed him. At last, a perfect client! Not one of the Precepts of Honorable Robbery applied to him; I had no compunction whatever. In fact, I enjoyed it. Better yet, that villain's cash was the foundation of our fortune. Of course, if you look closely enough, most fortunes have robbery of one sort or another at the bottom."

"With Master Hong's money, we bought a carriage and pair of horses," Mafoo said. "We thought that would be quicker than tramping through the country-side. We bought new clothes, too. No use rousing suspicion that we were vagrants. In fact, we looked so prosperous and substantial that I was able to do a little business here and there. For a while, we had a finger in the dumpling trade, with a handsome return on the investment. Trying to follow you from one place to another, we bought bolts of cloth, pots, pans, and such and sold them at an excellent profit. Had we kept on, we'd have made our fortunes a couple times over.

"It's mostly thanks to this long-legged lunatic," Mafoo continued. "He turned out to be a better businessman than he ever was a robber."

"It's the Eye of Discerning Perception," Moxa said, beaming proudly. "And the Nose of Thoughtful Inhalations. They served me well in ferreting out lucrative enterprises. I'm thinking seriously of giving up robbery and becoming a merchant. In business, there are no Precepts whatever to inconvenience you."

"You pair of rascals!" Jen burst out laughing. "To think I was ready to give you up for drowned! I wish I'd done as well as the two of you.

"As for me," Jen said, after telling what had befallen him, "the gifts for Yuan-ming are gone. Voyaging Moon may still have the flute. Whether she does or doesn't makes no difference. All I want is to find her. With the three of us together now, we can surely do that."

"Don't think we haven't tried," Mafoo said. "We searched for her as hard as we searched for you. She was here in Nang-pei until winter. We talked to the theater director. He couldn't help us. He had no idea where she went."

"Then we'll keep looking," Jen said. "I'll need clothes, to begin with. You have a carriage and horses? We can start off today."

"That won't be possible," Mafoo said.

"Why not?" returned Jen. "What's to stop us?"

"We'll not give up searching," Mafoo said, "but it must be put off a while. Before that, you must go to Ch'ang-an. As quickly as possible."

"What?" exclaimed Jen. "No, no, I see no use—"

"My plump friend is correct," put in Moxa. "The Heart of Sentimental Sympathy grieves for you. The Voice of Stern Practicality tells me you must do as he says."

Jen looked from Moxa to Mafoo. "I don't understand."

Mafoo's face was grave. "We heard of this a short while ago. Your honored father fell ill soon after you left the Celestial Palace. At the end of last week, the worthy man joined his honorable ancestors."

"My father—dead?" Jen gave an anguished cry. "And I not with him! No, not true."

"Alas, it is," Mafoo said quietly. "You are no longer Young Lord Prince. You are King of T'ang."

* * * * *

From wretched prisoner to King of T'ang! What will Jen do in these new circumstances? What of his beloved Voyaging Moon? This, and more, is told in the following chapter.

28

THREE MERCHANTS LEFT NANG-PEI at dawn. The innkeeper felt sorry to see them go. They had paid handsomely for services required. One had been ill but was now recovered, and all had set off south on business. What their business was, the innkeeper neither knew nor cared.

He did wonder, idly and briefly, why these gentlemen traveled without servants or carriage driver. The stubby, paunchy one took the reins himself and seemed quite skilled at it. The innkeeper did not inquire why he performed a task more befitting a groom or household servant. The long-legged one struck the innkeeper as a trifle eccentric, ever muttering about his nose and ears. But, wealthy guests were entitled to be eccentric.

As for the youngest, he said little, appearing withdrawn; the result, no doubt, of illness. A junior colleague, the innkeeper assumed, not having been informed that the young man happened to be the new king of T'ang.

This secrecy had been Jen's choice. As he told Mafoo and Moxa, the last thing in the world he wanted was to proclaim his identity.

"Without proof?" Jen said. "Whenever I tell anybody who I am, either they take me for a madman or I end up in trouble. Can you see us walking into an official's yamen and trying to convince him? He'd throw us all in prison, or worse."

Mafoo disagreed. "The palace has to know you're alive and on your way back. Otherwise, the ministers and councillors will be flapping around, making a mess of things. No telling what those fools will be up to. We'll send word. Privately."

Jen finally consented. At their first halt after leaving Nang-pei, he wrote a message in accordance with Mafoo's suggestion. Mafoo picked out a sturdy, reliable-looking fellow among the servants at the village inn, bought him a horse, handed him a purse of money, and ordered him to ride for Ch'ang-an as fast as he could.

"He'll be there well ahead of us," Mafoo said. "Since he can't read or write, he has no idea what he's carrying and won't gossip about it along the way. He'll do as he's told, he won't make off with the horse and money because he knows he'll be paid again doubly once he reaches the palace."

"Excellent plan," put in Moxa. "Greed will keep him honest."

Jen was satisfied with that. And not satisfied at all.

"Do I return as a king? No, I return as a failure," Jen said, in bitter self-reproach. "My father depended on me, but I turned away from my journey. The gifts he entrusted to me are lost, every one. I've even lost Voyaging Moon."

"You'll find your flute girl," Mafoo insisted. "You have royal power now. Once home, you can order searches in every corner of T'ang. Notify every official in every yamen. She's bound to turn up somewhere sooner or later."

"We might even come across her on the way," added Moxa. "The Nose, the Ear, the Eye are devoted to your service. In short, I'll keep on the lookout for her."

Jen had to admit that Mafoo was right. As king, Jen commanded more resources than before. The sooner in Ch'ang-an, the sooner he could use them.

In all haste to reach the capital, Jen urged Mafoo to continue on the roads past nightfall and to set off again before daybreak, with fresh horses wherever they could be found. Sometimes they galloped long stretches without a halt, one taking the reins while the other two slept. Near the end of their longest day, the weary travelers came in sight of the Lotus Bridge and the city's outskirts.

"Our messenger got there safely." Mafoo pulled up the horses. "We're expected. Look, they've sent an escort to welcome us. Out with you, Divine Majesty, and submit to the formal greetings."

Moxa had leaped from the carriage and was eagerly beckoning to the escort by the time Jen climbed down. With Mafoo beside him, Jen stood, hands in sleeves, while the warriors galloped toward them.

"Are you Jen Shao-yeh?" The troop captain reined up his mount. "The Young Lord Prince?"

Before Jen could answer, Mafoo stepped forward.

"No, he is not," Mafoo indignantly retorted. "What discourtesy is this? Dismount, captain. Pay respect properly. He is no longer Young Lord Prince, but His Divine Majesty Jen."

The troop captain seemed familiar. Jen had seen him before. Among the palace guard? Li Kwang's warriors? The memory teased and eluded him.

"There is no such ruler," the officer replied.

Jen suddenly recalled the cavern, the bandits. The man had been one of the Yellow Scarves. Jen cried a warning to Mafoo and Moxa. Too late. The troop had surrounded them.

"There is only one king of T'ang." The warrior drew his sword. "King Natha."

The prisoners were to be granted indulgence by the grace and generosity of Natha, King of T'ang. The troop captain informed them of this as they were herded under guard into the Celestial Palace, down corridors usually bustling with officials but now empty and echoing.

"Indulgence?" muttered Mafoo. "Grace and generosity? We're prisoners no matter how you look at it."

"He's doing us the favor of keeping us alive, I suppose," Jen said. "He could have had us killed out of hand."

"Then," Mafoo remarked, "be sure he's saving us for something equally nasty."

"The Nose of Suspicion failed," Moxa groaned. "I should have smelled a trap."

"Natha would have caught us sooner or later," Jen consoled the dismayed robber. "As we're alive, we may still have a chance."

They halted at a heavy door where two warriors stood guard. The troop captain unbolted it and gestured for them to enter. The portal swung shut behind them. The lamplight showed chambers sparsely furnished. The room held another occupant.

"Young Lord! Why did you not tell me who you were?"

An old woman hobbled toward Jen, who stared a moment before recognizing her. "Plum Blossom?"

"You brought my Fragrance of Orchid to life again." Plum Blossom would have kowtowed, but Jen took her hands in his own.

"The child is well, then?"

"Your gift restored her," Plum Blossom said, "and she flew away with it. Even so, I must believe she lives, happy wherever she may be."

The old woman's words puzzled him as much as her presence here. Jen asked no further explanation. His eyes had gone to the slender figure who had stepped from the adjoining chamber.

He cried out as Voyaging Moon ran to him. His months in the cangue, his hopeless searching, his failed journey all vanished from his mind. Mafoo's eyes popped, Moxa grinned all over his face.

"The Heart of Devotion swells!" exclaimed the Mad Robber. "The Eye of Tender Affection sheds a tear of joy—but if your sweetheart's in the palace, Your Majesty, it occurs to me she's a captive as much as we are."

"I couldn't warn you," Voyaging Moon said. "Natha told me you were on your way. The message you sent fell into his hands. He and his warriors had already captured the palace. They attacked Ch'ang-an when your father died. Plum Blossom and I had no chance to escape.

"Natha had secret dealings with some of the officials, so I heard," Voyaging Moon went on. "They practically invited him in. As for you, they thought they were well rid of you. They knew you were supposed to learn how Yuan-ming governed his kingdom and do likewise in T'ang. A king who knew how to rule was the last thing they wanted. They were afraid you'd be wise enough to kick them all out. Natha promised them—"

"That makes no difference now," Jen broke in. "We have to find a way out. We're together. That's all that matters. I lost you once. I won't lose you again. For the rest, for the palace, for Ch'ang-an, for the Kingdom of T'ang, I don't care—"

"You have to care," Voyaging Moon said. "You're king, not Natha. You know what he is. A brute and a killer. He forced you to give up the sword. Will you let him take your people, too?"

"Can I stop him?" Jen returned. "Any more than I stopped him from taking Yuan-ming's gift?"

"I don't know," Voyaging Moon said, "but you'd better start thinking about it. And about your father. He never lost hope that you'd come back. He counted on you to rule wisely in his place. I told him I knew you would. He was happy with that, and at peace—"

"You saw my father? You were here, then—?"

"I was with him when he died," Voyaging Moon said quietly. "I told him about our betrothal. He was glad. He gave us his blessing. Yes, I came to Ch'ang-an," she went on. "I'd been looking everywhere for you. Finally, I knew I couldn't find you on my own. I needed more help. I thought your father could give it. And so he'd have done, had there been time."

"I'm surprised they let you into the palace," Mafoo put in. "You've no idea how hard it is to gain an audience."

"Not for Lady Shadow Behind a Screen." Voyaging Moon grinned immodestly. "Her reputation traveled as fast as she did. The famous, mysterious flute girl? With news of the Young Lord Prince? They fell all over themselves opening the gates.

"And you, dearest Jen," Voyaging Moon continued, turning to him, "I played for you wherever I went, hoping you'd hear. Now I wish I hadn't. Because all it did was draw Natha's attention. He knew of Lady Shadow Behind a Screen. To find her in the palace— what an unexpected prize for him! All the more since he remembered me from the cavern. He remembered me all too well. Pig! He really gloated over finding me again. He's been keeping me under lock and key. Plum Blossom, too."

Voyaging Moon put a hand on the old woman's arm. "Poor soul, I saw her limping along the road, in the midst of a snowstorm. I took her into my carriage. She told me about her granddaughter. And the young stranger who gave her a kite. So I knew at least you hadn't drowned in the Lo. I meant to do Plum Blossom a service, taking her with me to Ch'ang-an, to get help from your father. Now she's in the same pickle as we are."

"Natha has no grievance against her," Jen said. "Why should he do her any harm? For myself, that's a different matter. He'll have to get rid of me. I'm surprised he hasn't done it already. I'm surprised he even let me see you. He's not one to do favors."

"That," said Voyaging Moon, "was my idea. I struck a bargain with him. He agreed to give me a few hours with you. Royally generous! He thinks himself quite the king, but he's still the same arrogant ruffian. Worse. He's gone a little mad on top of everything else. I've heard he talks to his sword. He struts and preens enough to turn your stomach. He wanted an ornament for the palace, something to flaunt and boast about. In this case: Lady Shadow Behind a Screen.

"That's my part of the bargain," Voyaging Moon added. "I told him I'd marry him."

• • • • •

Noble sacrifice! Terrible bargain! Has Jen found Voyaging Moon only to lose her, along with his life? What hope at all for him? Can a desperate situation turn worse? It can and does. To learn how, go on to the next chapter.

29

• Voyaging Moon breaks a bargain •
• The Mad Robber offers a plan •
• King Natha and King Jen •

"HUSH, HUSH. IT WON'T HAPPEN." Voyaging Moon put a hand on Jen's lips. "Do you think I'd keep a bargain like that? Natha gave me what I wanted. He'll get nothing back for it.

"I wanted you with me, and so you are," Voyaging Moon went on. "I wanted time. We have some. Not much. But if I can stretch it out, we might have a chance. The longer you stay alive, the better chance we'll have."

"How can there be any chance at all?" Jen said. "Time? Time for what?"

"Natha calls himself King of T'ang," Voyaging Moon said. "He isn't. I've heard things since I've been here. The northern province is rallying against him. It started last winter. One village held him off. That heartened other villages. Now, half the districts are up in arms. He's had to send most of his warriors north. They put down one uprising, another starts. He's bitten off more than he can chew. King? Yes, in Ch'ang-an and some of the outlying towns. Even there, he's stretched too thin."

"That's all as may be," Mafoo put in. "What's happening someplace else doesn't do anything for us here. That turtle has the palace. Worse, he has us inside it."

"So, the more delay the better," Voyaging Moon said. She turned back to Jen. "You have more friends than you think. Not all the officials took up with Natha. Some turned out surprisingly honest and spoke against him. It cost their lives. A lot of others are on your side, but they're too terrified to say anything. Once word spreads that you're here, they could try to help you. The palace troops have been disarmed. If they can get their weapons back—"

"If?" Jen said, with a bleak smile. "So many 'if's. If I hadn't fished Master Fu out of the river? If we hadn't gone searching for Li Kwang? And still another 'if.' If you can't put off Natha? If he forces the marriage?"

"I've thought of that, too," Voyaging Moon said. "He's let me have serving women. I talked one of them into giving me this."

The girl reached into her jacket and brought out a dagger. "At the ceremony, as soon as I'm close enough to him—"

"No," Jen said. "His guards would kill you an instant later. No. I can't let you try."

"Dear Jen," Voyaging Moon answered, "you may not be in a position to say much about it."

"It's a fine scheme!" exclaimed Moxa. "I see it now! The wedding ritual cut short—for Natha, in every sense of the word. But the unwilling bride won't be our lovely flute girl. It will be: myself!

"I'll be robed and veiled," Moxa hurried on. "Your serving women will help with that, won't they? I'll have the dagger ready to hand. Then, I step up to embrace that villain—"

Voyaging Moon smiled and shook her head. "Moxa, you're a lunatic. A courageous one, and we love you. But, for one thing, you can't pass yourself off as me, no matter how you dress up. For another, you'll end up dead. For still another, your arithmetic's bad. One captive missing? What will I be doing in the meantime? What does Natha have in store for the rest of you?"

"Correct," said Mafoo. "That scheme's ridiculous on the very face of it. If we try anything, we try to get ourselves out of here. I've been calculating exactly where we are."

"We aren't near the royal apartments," Jen said. "I don't know this wing of the palace."

"I do," Mafoo said. "Inner chambers. At ground level. Beyond that wall should be arcades, the Gardens of Tranquil Delight—"

"Utterly simple!" cried Moxa. "Why didn't you say that before? You forget I was a professional robber before I took up an easier trade. Here, let me have that dagger."

Voyaging Moon handed him the blade. At Moxa's instruction, Jen and Mafoo tore down the draperies covering the wall. Mafoo eyed the heavy stones.

"Robber or not, you can't dig your way through that."

"Of course I can." Moxa rolled up his sleeves. "There's always a weak spot somewhere. If I chip away the mortar, get one stone loose—"

Jen watched doubtfully as the robber scraped and scratched at the unyielding wall. Mafoo glanced at Jen and shook his head. Undaunted, Moxa kept on.

"The Hand of Consummate Skill," declared the robber. "The Spirit of Patient Determination—"

The blade snapped.

Moxa stared, crestfallen. "Ah—yes, the Hand might have gone at it a little too vigorously."

"Let it be," Jen said. "We can't do anything from inside. We'll need help from outside. You have serving women?" he asked Voyaging Moon. "Could they get word to an official we trust?"

"Possibly," Voyaging Moon said. "They come in the mornings. I don't know if we dare wait that long."

"No choice," Mafoo said. "Keep thinking, meantime. Even Moxa might come up with a workable plan."

In the lamp-lit chamber, Jen could not tell night from day. As they settled themselves, Voyaging Moon brought out the flute and quietly played. Jen closed his eyes and listened gratefully, but his heart was heavy, scarcely open to the melody. For the few moments that he drowsed, he dreamed the wooden collar hung once again around his neck.

He started up. The lamps guttered. The door had flung open. Armed warriors were upon them, seizing Jen, surrounding Voyaging Moon and the others.

"Stand away. Let him face me."

Natha swaggered into the chamber. The bandit glittered in full armor. At his side hung the sword destined for Yuan-ming.

Natha put his hands on his hips and looked Jen up and down. His eyes glittered like his breastplate. "You told the truth when last we met. If I'd known you were a royal whelp, you wouldn't be alive at this moment. For all that, you served me well. The sword you gave me—unwillingly, but you gave it nonetheless—that sword and I are close comrades." Natha glanced at the weapon. "Aren't we, my thirsty friend? Together, we rule."

"Bandit then, bandit now," Jen replied. "Your kingdom's narrow as the edge of your blade."

"Is it?" Natha grinned. "I don't think so. Oh, no,

my lad, I don't think so at all. Your gift turned out more interesting than you might have known. I spared your life in exchange for it. That was a mistake. No matter, it will be corrected. You'll soon count yourself among your ancestors."

The terror which had threatened to drown Jen in the cavern began rising. Yet, as he raised his head to meet Natha's eyes, the tide ebbed and drained away. He could see the man before him as no more than a grotesque, posturing shadow, weightless, without substance. Jen looked at him with contempt and with a strange pity. "You have already lost. You have lost without knowing it.

"Do you remember Ping-erh? I thought I failed. Perhaps I did. But others did not. Pebbles stopped the avalanche. In the end, they will break you, and you will break yourself on them."

Natha's hand went to his sword. Foam flecks came to his lips. Jen thought the man would strike him down where he stood. Natha ground his teeth and drew a great breath. His glance wavered. He turned away to fix on Voyaging Moon.

"Lady Shadow Behind a Screen. You and I have a bargain."

"Broken," Voyaging Moon said. "Broken even as I made it."

"You'll keep it," Natha said, with a cold smile. "Willing or not." He turned to Mafoo and Moxa. "You'll follow your master."

Mafoo shrugged. "As I've always done."

"The Sinews of Courage!" cried Moxa. "The Heart of Devotion will not falter!"

"You think not?" Natha said. "Poor fools, both of you. Have you seen a man killed? A head roll in the dirt? Oh, you will. You'll smell real blood. Then find out how long your bravery lasts. I'll hear you scream for mercy."

"Let the old woman go," Jen said. "She has no part in this."

"She does," Natha said. "I want her alive, a hostage to guarantee the flute girl's good behavior." He motioned to the warriors. "Take them. The headsman waits."

Before Jen could embrace his beloved for the last time, he was marched from the chamber. Mafoo and Moxa, Plum Blossom and Voyaging Moon were prodded along behind him, out of the palace and through the Jade Gate.

Men at arms hedged the square. In the pale morning light, a crowd had gathered, held back by spearmen and archers. Many there had seen the Young Lord Prince depart happily from the city, and they had cheered him. Now they stood mute with despair. Two of Natha's guards seized Jen, led him a little distance from the gate, and halted him before the executioner.

The headsman gestured for the guards to stand aside. He seized the condemned man by the hair and forced him to his knees, then brought up a long-bladed sword.

Weapon poised, he tightened his grip on the hilt. Out-cries rose from the crowd. The executioner hesitated.

"Strike!" Natha's voice rang out.

Sword raised, the executioner stood as if frozen. His eyes had turned from his victim to the far fringe of the crowd. The cries spread, swelling to wild screams. Low rumbling filled the air. The executioner's mouth fell open. He stared in terror and disbelief.

The crowd parted. Onlookers flung themselves aside, scattering to make way for a column of horsemen and foot soldiers. The ground shook beneath the tread of the approaching warriors. Unswerving, step by step, they moved across the square: not men, but statues sprung to life.

The warriors were of solid stone.

Leading them, his granite features set in grim deter-mination, eyes \blazing with the cold brilliance of dia-monds, rode Li Kwang. Having struggled from the cavern, obeying the instructions of Master Wu, he and his troop had borne steadily toward Ch'ang-an. Day after day, month after month, in summer sun and win-ter snow, they held their slow and agonizing course. Through mountain passes, trackless forests, every inch seeming a mile, Autumn Dew had never faltered, nor had Li Kwang lost hope. Now, at last, Li Kwang had reached his goal.

He and his troop pressed forward. At sight of them, Natha's guards attempted to hold them off, raining vol-ley after volley of arrows on the cavalcade. The shafts rattled and glanced off; the warriors never halted their inexorable advance. On they came, while spears shattered against their stone breasts. Horses' hooves and booted feet pounded a relentless rhythm. Threatening to crush all who stood in their path, the warriors drew ever closer. No beings of mere flesh and blood could resist this massive onslaught, like a glacier on the march. Seeing attack was hopeless and defense impossible, Natha's guards broke ranks and fled.

"Strike!" Natha roared again. "Strike now!"

But the executioner had already raced away in panic. Spitting curses, Natha snatched his sword from its scabbard. Glimpsing Li Kwang, Jen sprang to his feet. By then, Natha was upon him, kicking him to the ground, raising the sword high in both hands to sweep it downward.

• • • • •

Has Li Kwang come too late? Will nothing save Jen? Those who care to know what happens should go quickly to the following chapter.

30

THEY FOLLOWED THE RISING SUN. With Niang-niang, the great eagle, at her side, Fragrance of Orchid sailed amid shafts of light. The kite bore the girl on the wind tides, up the slopes and down the valleys of air currents. She had learned to guide the kite, to fly as skillfully and swiftly as Niang-niang. Laughing, she plunged down through the clouds. Niang-niang beat her powerful wings to catch up with the child.

They swooped lower. Fragrance of Orchid glimpsed rooftops, streets, and bridges. Tall towers, flashing golden, caught her eye. She veered to hover above them.

"The Celestial Palace in Ch'ang-an," the eagle told her.

"How beautiful!" exclaimed Fragrance of Orchid. "We've never been here before. Oh, Niang-niang, I must have a closer look!"

Fragrance of Orchid dropped earthward. "See all the people in the square," she called to Niang-niang. "Is it a festival? But why are soldiers holding them back? And there, what are those? Can they be statues?" She caught her breath in astonishment. "Yes, warriors of stone," she gasped, "but they're marching! Marching into the square!

"And there's a man holding a big sword. And someone's being dragged in front of him. What's happening?" Fragrance of Orchid narrowed her eyes and sharpened her vision. "Niang-niang, I know who he is! He gave me this kite!"

Fragrance of Orchid's gaze fell on other figures. "I see Grandmother Plum Blossom! How has she come here? Why are soldiers around her? No matter, I've found her. You said I would, if that's where my path led. Come, fly down with me."

"I am not permitted," said Niang-niang. "You, yes. Fly, if you wish, as fast as you can. Your grandmother is being held captive. The stranger who gave you the kite is the rightful King of T'ang. He has been condemned to death."

"We have to save them both," cried Fragrance of Orchid. "Please, Niang-niang, please help me. I need you more than ever."

"I cannot do as you ask," replied the eagle. "You have come to the end of your journey, if indeed you choose to end it. But I must tell you this: If you set foot upon the ground here, then you and I must part forever. And you, child, will never fly aloft, except in dreams."

Though fearing her heart would break, Fragrance of Orchid hesitated less than an instant. "Farewell—farewell, dear Niang-niang."

"Farewell, dear child of air and earth."

Only once did Fragrance of Orchid look back for a last glimpse of Niang-niang. But the great golden eagle had vanished.

Jen thought it was a huge bird swooping from the sky. Then he realized it was a kite with a child clinging to it. That same moment, plummeting at top speed, Fragrance of Orchid flung herself upon Natha before he could swing the sword. The girl's attack threw him off balance, and he staggered back, half-stunned.

Jen sprang up. Believing him safe, the girl gave a cry of joy and ran to the arms of Plum Blossom. Voyaging Moon, Mafoo, and Moxa sped to Jen's side.

But Natha would not be cheated of his victim. Roaring, brandishing the sword, he set straight for Jen.

"To Li Kwang!" Jen shouted, thinking to take refuge amid the ranks of stone warriors.

Natha's guards, however, fearing their chieftain's wrath more than Li Kwang's grim troop, plucked up their courage and regrouped, blocking the path of the escaping prisoners.

"This way!" Mafoo gestured frantically. "Li Kwang will deal with those fellows. Out of here! Out of Natha's reach!"

Mafoo raced from the square. Jen and Voyaging Moon, with Moxa loping beside them, followed. Natha, in hot pursuit, was at their heels, gaining ground as they plunged down a narrow street and swung around a corner.

Had Mafoo sought to escape through the twisting lanes and alleys, his plan failed. Natha, maddened with rage, still followed. Moxa, shouting for his companions to press on, halted and tried to fling himself on their pursuer. Eyes only on Jen, Natha lunged past Moxa, sending him head over heels, and doubled his pace. In moments, he would be within striking distance. Natha tightened his grip on the sword. Ahead, Jen faltered for an instant. Natha shouted in triumph.

It had been a long journey for Master Chu. From the day he picked up the bronze bowl at the riverbank, he had turned his steps southward. All through the winter, he made his way along snow-drifted roads, plodding from village to village, town to town, sleeping in doorways or under bridges. Sleet froze in his beard, wind buffeted him but he continued nevertheless. Though he asked for no alms, many folk felt strangely drawn to him and eager to fill his bowl. Some offered him shelter in their homes. He smiled, thanked them kindly but shook his head and continued on his way.

At last, one morning, Master Chu came to Ch'ang-an. The streets were nearly empty. Most of the townspeople had gone to the square in front of the Celestial Palace. Master Chu did not join them. Instead, he hobbled down a twisting lane not far from the palace.

Turning a corner, he stopped short. Several people raced toward him. Master Chu stepped aside as Jen and his companions sped past. Close behind them came an armored man wielding a sword.

"Natha Yellow Scarf," Master Chu called out, "you easily broke an earthen bowl. Let us see what you can do to bronze."

He flung the bowl at Natha's feet, tripping him and sending him pitching headlong.

Natha scrambled up almost immediately and resumed the chase, but his victims had for the moment outdistanced him. Master Chu retrieved the bowl and hobbled after them.

In the Happy Phoenix Gardens, an individual wearing a felt cap with earflaps sat at a folding table, an umbrella beside him. Chen-cho had fulfilled one of his ambitions. He had long dreamed of seeing the famous gardens. At last, he had made his way there, arriving just in time to catch the morning light. Next to him, as was his habit now, he had set up the landscape he had painted months before in a village called Ping-erh. Chen-cho had dipped his brush and begun to work. He stopped in midstroke.

"Now, what the devil is this?" Chen-cho had hoped to be undisturbed, but several people were streaking in his direction. Why they were running at such speed and what their purposes might be were none of his business. He started back to his painting. He looked again and set down the brush.

"Why—it's Ragbag! That rascal! Oho, I see what this is all about." Chen-cho chuckled to himself. "He's run off with a girl. And two friends helping them elope. And here comes her angry father. In a fine fury, I'd say. He's got a sword—"

The painter's amusement suddenly vanished when he saw the pursuer was Natha Yellow Scarf.

"Ragbag! Ragbag! Here!" Chen-cho shouted. He turned to the painting beside him. "Quick! Lao-hu!"

Even when he had time to think about it, Jen could not entirely piece together what happened so quickly. First, he heard Chen-cho calling him. He halted and spun around, only to find Natha behind him.

Jen flung up his arms. Teeth bared, eyes blazing, Natha raised the sword for a last killing stroke. That instant, Jen believed he heard a voice cry out:

"Give me no more to drink!"

The blade shuddered and twisted like a living thing and wrested itself from Natha's hands. Despite his bewilderment, Jen snatched up the fallen blade.

At the same time, across the garden paths bounded an enormous tiger.

Natha fell back, lurched away, and sped down one of the paths, the huge animal at his heels.

"Lao-hu!" Chen-cho shouted and waved his arms. "To me!"

With the tiger snarling behind him, Natha was driven toward the artist, who was holding up a painting.

"Hurry, Natha!" cried Chen-cho. "Into the woods! Jump!"

Before Jen could swallow his astonishment at seeing the artist, let alone the sudden appearance of a furious tiger, he was astonished again. For the next thing he saw, though he could not believe his eyes, was Natha plunging into what Jen took for a painted landscape. The tiger leaped after him. Both vanished.

By this time, with Moxa and Mafoo at her side, Voyaging Moon had run to Jen, who stared dumbfounded while Chen-cho laughed and clapped him on the shoulder.

"Never fear, Honorable Ragbag. I don't think that villain will be back."

Jen rubbed his eyes. "Chen-cho? What are you telling me? Where's Natha? For a minute, I'd have sworn I saw him jump into that picture."

"Oh, he did. He did, indeed," replied Chen-cho. "I'll tell you about that later. One thing I can promise you now. He's not where he'd like to be. If he's anywhere at all."

Chen-cho held the painting for the baffled Jen to examine. "Nice, isn't it? Lovely landscape, best I've done. Thanks to the brush and ink stone you gave me. Look closer. You might see a friend of mine." Chen-cho bent and called out, "Lao-hu? Are you busy?"

Jen peered at the beautiful scene of meadows and forests. Voyaging Moon was the first to notice, and she pointed to a thicket of greenery. Gazing out from it, orange eyes aglow, was the head of a tiger contentedly licking his chops.

"No question," said Chen-cho. "Natha won't be back."

Jen had still digested none of this when a horseman cantered up and sprang from the saddle.

"Li Kwang!" Jen stared at him. "In the square—I saw you and your men. As if you were stone statues—"

"Stone once, but no longer," Li Kwang replied. "A promise has been made and kept. Much has happened to us, but for now you need only know this: Master Wu found us trapped in Mount Wu-shan. He told me that if I and my men could reach Ch'ang-an, and you still lived, we would again be flesh and blood. And so it has come to pass. I failed once in my duty toward you. I have not failed again."

Jen, during this, caught sight of an old man limping toward him. "Master Chu?" He would have gone to the beggar, but Li Kwang raised a hand.

"My warriors have armed the household troops. Natha's men have fled, all who lived to do so. Go immediately to the Celestial Palace, Your Majesty."

"What did he say?" murmured Chen-cho. "Your Majesty? King Ragbag?"

"Something like that." Jen grinned. "Come with us. And bring your tiger."

They gathered in the Great Hall of Audience. On the Dragon Throne, Voyaging Moon beside him, with Mafoo and Moxa close by, Jen listened with ever-growing amazement to each account of the objects he had given during his journey.

Li Kwang had brought the saddle with him. He laid it at Jen's feet.

"This is not mine to ride," Li Kwang said, "and so I return it to you."

Master Chu held out the bronze bowl. "This belongs in your Hall of Priceless Treasures, and I have brought it here."

"Your kite let me fly, as I always wished," said Fragrance of Orchid, leaving Plum Blossom's embrace to stand before Jen. "Now it's yours again."

"I'll say likewise for the brush and ink stone," put in Chen-cho. "I painted as I never painted before. Even so, I can manage well enough without them."

"No," Jen said, looking at each in turn. "You must keep them. All that was given has come back to me, but I give them again to each of you. Were they valuable objects when I first set out with them? No, I think not. You have made them so. Gifts? You offered me gifts greater than ever I gave you: friendship, devotion, help when I most needed it. Only the sword will be kept, and locked away, for I do not intend to use it."

"What about the flute?" Voyaging Moon said, with a teasing smile. "Lady Shadow Behind a Screen hasn't offered to give it back. I suppose I should."

"Never." Jen smiled back. "Master Wu said it was a gift for Yuan-ming. I believe he made a mistake. It was yours, always, from the first."

"I think you're right," said Voyaging Moon.

* * * * *

Happy end at last! Not yet. Those who have come this far have read tales of six valuable objects. Now, Jen must have a tale of his own, and it will be found in the next chapter.

31

• The Tale of King Jen
and the Second Journey •

KING JEN AND PRECIOUS CONSORT VOYAGING MOON
governed happily and wisely in the Kingdom of T'ang.
Their chief councillor was a good-natured, practical-
minded fellow named Mafoo, who had served his master from the days when King Jen was still the Young
Lord Prince. First Official of the Treasury was a re-
formed robber, Moxa, who was best able to keep an
eye open for possible thieves.

Once, long before, when he was a young man, Jen
had set out for the marvelous realm of T'ien-kuo. He

had never reached his destination and he regretted it. He still remembered the vow he had made to himself on a bleak road in the northern province to continue his journey with Voyaging Moon. Yet, each time he thought he might keep that promise, he found himself always too occupied with other matters of benefit to his own kingdom.

And so the years passed. Jen and Voyaging Moon raised many sons and daughters. The people of T'ang were as happy as their rulers. They thrived and prospered, the land yielded harvests in abundance, the arts flourished as richly as the orchards. The laws that King Jen devised were just, but seldom enforced, since Jen encouraged his subjects to deal with each other as they themselves would wish to be dealt with. Few officials were needed, but they served their monarch and the people well.

At last, Jen saw that the best moment had come, and he resolved to set out once again for T'ien-kuo.

"From what you once told me," Precious Consort Voyaging Moon said, "we can't go empty-handed to the palace of Yuan-ming."

"True," King Jen said, "but we shall go empty-handed nevertheless. Since I do not know what to offer, I shall carry nothing at all.

"The great Yuan-ming will not grant us audience, nor shall I seek one. I wish only to see his kingdom with my own eyes. In that way, perhaps, I may learn how better to govern T'ang."

Voyaging Moon agreed. So, leaving the Celestial Palace in the good care of Mafoo, Moxa, and the steadfast general, Broken Face Kwang, they traveled northward, as Jen had done so long ago.

Jen and Voyaging Moon drove their carriage themselves, taking no escort or entourage, knowing they would be welcomed and received with affection at every stop along the way.

However, scarcely a full day from Ch'ang-an, they halted. In the road ahead stood an old man, white-haired, barefoot, leaning on a staff.

"Can that be Master Wu?" Jen climbed from the carriage and, with Voyaging Moon, hurried to greet him.

"No, it's not Master Wu," Jen said, drawing nearer. "It's Master Fu. No, it's Master Shu. Or—can that be Master Chu?"

It was none of them. It was Master Hu, his beloved teacher who, years before, had vanished from the palace.

Jen gave a joyful cry and ran to embrace him. "Dear Master! What happy chance to find you. But— here? Of all times and places."

"Time and place are not important," replied Master Hu, beaming. "Indeed, I get myself constantly mixed up in them; I can never be certain which is which, where or when, and so I ignore them. As for chance, my boy, is there such a thing? Do we call 'chance' only what we cannot foresee?

"If we look backward instead of forward," he went on, "might we not discover that one thing set in motion sets all else moving? Tug the edge of a spiderweb and the center moves. But I have no intention of lecturing you. Tell me, rather, why you have left your palace."

Jen recounted what had befallen him during his first journey and explained the purpose of his second.

Master Hu shook his head. "My dear boy, have I failed in your instruction? Have I not taught you to avoid useless pursuits and the pointless waste of time?

"An old tale tells of a traveler who kept walking northward," Master Hu continued. "At last, he returned to the spot where he began. The Kingdom of T'ienkuo? If, indeed, such a realm exists, it is any place you make it to be. Therefore, why seek what you have already found?"

Jen puzzled over this. By the time he grasped what Master Hu meant by it, Voyaging Moon had already understood. Smiling lovingly, she took Jen's arm.

"Come, dear Jen," she said. "Come home. If, that is, we ever truly left it."

And that was exactly what they did.

· · · · ·